W9-DFQ-291

DISCARD

Applebaum's Garage

Applebaum's Garage

BY KAREN LYNN WILLIAMS

CLARION BOOKS/*New York*

Clarion Books
a Houghton Mifflin Company imprint
215 Park Avenue South, New York, NY 10003
Text copyright © 1993 by Karen Lynn Williams

Library of Congress Cataloging-in-Publication Data

Williams, Karen Lynn.
Applebaum's garage / by Karen Lynn Williams.
p.   cm.
Summary: When his best friend Robbie starts acting
strange and hanging around older boys, ten-year-old Jeremy
spends more and more time next door with old Mr. Applebaum,
whose ability to fix anything has filled his garage and yard
with amazing junk.
ISBN 0-395-65227-8
[1. Friendship—Fiction.   2. Old age—Fiction.]   I.
Title.
PZ7.W66655Ap   1994
[Fic]—dc20   92-31336
                                                        CIP
                                                         AC

BP   10   9   8   7   6   5   4   3   2   1

For the Rawson family,
with gratitude

Applebaum's Garage

<u>Chapter</u> 1

Jeremy ran all the way home from the bus stop after school on Monday. The first day back after spring vacation was hot for early April and he felt the sweat bead up along his hairline, but he ran until he reached the edge of his yard. He just wanted to get over to Applebaum's and forget about stupid Robbie Fuller.

Jeremy raced up the back steps and dumped his backpack full of books, papers, and lunch box on the kitchen counter. A slip of paper swooshed off the counter and sailed to the floor. Jeremy picked it up and read: "I'll be a little late. Home by four. Two cookies, milk, and fruit. Help yourself. Love, Mom. P.S. Leave a note if you go out. XOXO."

Jeremy grabbed two chocolate chip cookies from the cookie jar and shoved them whole into his mouth. Then he hurried upstairs. Mom had said it was too early to start wearing shorts because it was still cool in the morning, but now his legs itched and prickled with the heat. Jeremy kicked off his sneakers and pulled off his pants. He pulled a pair of shorts out of the drawer and slid them on. Stuffing his foot back into one shoe, he put the other one on, half hopping and half tripping out of the bedroom.

Jeremy thought about taking another cookie, but that meant he would need milk and he didn't have time. He was kind of glad Mom wasn't home yet. She would want to know where Robbie was, and Jeremy didn't feel like talking. She might even say he couldn't go to Applebaum's.

He ran down the back steps straightening the elastic waistband of his shorts. They felt baggy so he pulled them up a little. *Darn*, he thought, they were on backwards. The pocket should be in the back. So what? Mr. Applebaum didn't care about things like that.

"Boy, is that you sneaking through my hedges again?"

Jeremy started and turned to see skinny Mrs. Applebaum on her back steps. She was wiping her fingers on a flowered apron. Her stockings were tied down around her calves and her hair was pulled back in a bun.

"I wasn't sneaking, ma'am," Jeremy said politely.

"How many times do I have to tell you to stay away from my hedges?"

Jeremy just looked at the gray-haired woman and waited. Mr. Applebaum said his wife's bark was worse than her bite, and Jeremy knew they weren't her hedges anyway. His mom had planted them there years ago to hide the mess around Applebaum's garage, and she always said they were only now getting high enough to accomplish the job.

"Don't talk back to me, boy, you hear?" Mrs. Applebaum turned to go inside. "You tell that man to get me an egg or two from them chickens. I swear, can't never find a body when you need him," she grumbled.

After the bright sunlight outside, the garage was dark. Jeremy blinked and squinted. As his eyes began to adjust he could make out the dark form of Mr. Applebaum bent over an old wooden chair with a hammer in one hand. He was whistling softly between his teeth, like always, the same phrase over and over again. Jeremy often hummed the tune in his head. He thought of it as Mr. A.'s theme song. Now Jeremy could see

3

Mr. Applebaum's bushy silver white hair falling across his forehead as he leaned over his work.

Mr. Applebaum barely looked up from what he was doing. "Hey, son," he said.

"Hey," Jeremy answered. He took a deep breath and began to relax.

Applebaum's garage was his favorite place. In this one big room there was everything everyone wanted but couldn't find, and everything no one thought they needed. There were seven long hip boots hanging from the rafters. They were all different lengths and colors—green, black, and one was even yellow. The longest one just rubbed the top of Jeremy's head as he walked under it, making the hairs on his neck stand up. He crouched down next to a crate of old doorknobs. There were thirty-two different ones. Jeremy had counted them. Some were shiny brass, some were old and dull metal, and some were made of glass. He picked one up and spun it on the cement floor like a top.

In Applebaum's garage there were hundreds, maybe thousands, of nuts and bolts and nails and screws. There were ten different ladders, the last time Jeremy had counted. There were inner tubes and outer tires and all kinds of wires and ropes. Mr. Applebaum even had six hens in the garage that sometimes laid eggs. Jeremy never got tired of being with Mr. Applebaum in his garage. There was always something to do.

4

Today, Jeremy wanted to work on his fort, which was out behind the garage on the edge of the garden. He stepped out the side door and around the side of the old weathered building. He'd been working out here all vacation and he'd finished the whole project with stuff from the garage and only a little help from Mr. Applebaum.

First Jeremy had dug a hole deep enough to stand up in, almost, and wide enough for at least two people to lie down in. That had taken most of the week. Then Mr. Applebaum had helped him cover the hole with two old doors, which made the roof for Jeremy's fort. Jeremy had thought maybe he would camouflage the whole thing with dirt and branches so no one would know it was there. He had hoped Robbie would help with that. The best part was the trapdoor. It was an old pink toilet seat with a lid that rested on the end of one of the doors and the dirt at the edge of the hole, filling a space that the doors didn't quite cover. Jeremy could just fit through it if he made himself skinny by stretching out and sucking in his stomach, so he could use it to go in and out. He could also pop the seat open from inside to see what was outside.

Now Jeremy needed to finish putting tiles on the floor and walls of his fort. Mr. Applebaum had plenty in the garage, all sizes and colors. They were all pastels—blue, gray, green, and brown, speckled with darker shades. Jeremy headed back to the garage for more tiles. Something on Mr. Applebaum's workbench caught his eye.

"You found the mirrors," Jeremy exclaimed. He picked up a small one and grinned at himself. He stuck out his tongue and crossed his eyes, making a crazy face. His shiny, straight black hair covered his eyebrows and almost reached his brown eyes.

"Knew I had them here, somewhere," Mr. Applebaum said.

Jeremy watched as Mr. Applebaum sawed away at a piece of black plastic pipe. Then he fit three pieces together, one long straight piece and two short ones that were curved and a little wider. The short pieces fit on the ends of the long straight piece and stuck out in opposite directions.

"It's really going to work," Jeremy said. "A real periscope." Jeremy had gotten the idea last week and he had drawn a picture. His older sister, Andrea, had said it would never work, but when Jeremy had shown it to Mr. Applebaum, he said Jeremy was smart. A periscope was just what he needed for his fort in the ground.

Now Mr. Applebaum showed Jeremy how to cut the mirror with a special glass cutter. It made a line. Then Jeremy tapped the mirror and it divided into two pieces with perfectly straight edges. Mr. Applebaum made a groove in the pipes, set the mirrors in, and put the ends back on. Jeremy stuck one end of the periscope out the garage door and looked through the other end. It took him a minute to realize he was seeing the gate to the garden. "It works!" he shouted. "Thanks, Mr. Applebaum. I've got to try it in the fort." He headed out the door.

"Samuel. Sam-uuuu-ellll!" Mrs. Applebaum was half singing and half yelling for Mr. Applebaum the way she always did when she wanted him.

Jeremy went back to the garage. "She wants eggs," he said to his friend, hanging his head. "I forgot." He didn't want to get Mr. Applebaum into trouble.

"Don't worry about that," Mr. Applebaum said. "I'll get the eggs. You go out and try the scope." He winked at Jeremy.

Jeremy squeezed through the trapdoor and dropped into his fort. It was cool and damp. It smelled sweet and earthy. The tiles lining part of one wall looked great. Jeremy liked the light-green ones with brown specks best. He put the periscope up through the toilet seat opening and turned slowly around. All he could see were parts of things, but it was going to be great for playing submarine. *Better get to work*, Jeremy thought as he brought the scope in. He ran back to the garage and without getting sidetracked this time, he got the tiles and began laying them out a half inch apart and packed loose dirt in around them.

As he worked Jeremy realized he hadn't been thinking about Robbie. Robbie was Jeremy's best friend. He had been away at his dad's for the whole of spring vacation, and Jeremy had waited all week to tell him about the fort. But today at the bus stop, Robbie had said, "Forts are for babies." When they got on the bus, Robbie sat in the back with some noisy sixth-graders Jeremy knew only by sight. In school Robbie barely spoke to Jeremy at all, and at lunch recess he stayed over in one corner of the playground with the same sixth-grade boys.

Jeremy stepped back to admire his work. He shouldn't have told Robbie about his fort at all.

Suddenly the doors overhead began to rattle and shake. For a minute, Jeremy thought it was an earthquake. Then he heard, "Hey Squirt, you in there?"

It was Andrea. *Worse than an earthquake*, Jeremy thought.

"Cut that out," he yelled. "You'll break it."

Andrea opened up the toilet seat and stuck her head through the hole.

"I can't believe it. A sewer." Her black curls hung down into the fort. "Mom says to get home now. You didn't leave a note, and just because of you I had to get off the phone with Jamie and come out here to find you." She slammed the seat shut. Jeremy heard her walk back across the doors.

More like an elephant than an earthquake, Jeremy thought. Andrea was in the seventh grade, first year of middle school, and she thought she was hot stuff. She always had a phone stuck to her ear, and she'd started calling him Squirt, even though she was only two years older.

Jeremy sighed. He'd forgotten to leave a note, and Mom was going to be steaming. He grabbed his periscope, hoisted himself out of the trapdoor, and made a quick stop by the garage. "Gotta go," he called in the door.

"So I heard," Mr. Applebaum said. He waved to Jeremy and kept right on with what he was doing.

Jeremy held the periscope up. "Thanks again. It works great. Bye." Mrs. Applebaum was nowhere in sight, so he squeezed through the hedge, holding the periscope over his head.

"Hi, Mom," he said, coming into the kitchen. "How was work?" If he could get his mother started on another subject, maybe she'd forget to be mad or ask where he had been.

It didn't work. "Where have you been? You're filthy, dirt all over you. Look at those shorts! And they're on backwards."

Andrea came out of the hall closet. She took

the phone away from her ear long enough to say, "He's been playing in a huge pit, covered over with boards and junk, at the Applebaums'." She ducked back into the closet.

"Sounds dangerous," Mom said, frowning. "I'm afraid you'll hurt yourself over there. Maybe I'd better have a look at what you're up to."

"Mom, it's OK," Jeremy said. "Mr. Applebaum even helped me build a real periscope."

"Well, next time leave me a note," Mom said. "I wish you'd play with your friends more, though."

"Mr. Applebaum is my friend," Jeremy told her.

"Friends your own age," Mom said. "It's not healthy, hanging around with that old man all the time."

It's a lot better than hanging around with some friends my own age, Jeremy wanted to tell her.

"Where's Robbie today?" she continued. "He got back from his dad's yesterday, didn't he?"

"I'll go get washed up," Jeremy said. He didn't need Robbie and he didn't have to explain it to Mom.

Chapter 2

"So tell us about school today," Dad said that evening at dinner. "How was your first day back?"

"Great." Andrea started right away. "There's a new boy in the seventh grade. He's cute and he sits right next to me in science. Mr. Cummings asked me to share my book with him. And," she went on without even taking a breath, "I got an A on my science project."

Normally, Jeremy would have interrupted his sister just because she had such a big mouth, but today he was happy to let her do the talking.

"Well, Jeremy?" Dad asked after Andrea finally finished. "How was your day?"

11

"OK." Jeremy could tell he wasn't very convincing.

"Jeremy," Mom said. "What's the matter?"

"Nothing," Jeremy said. "This lasagna's great." He took another mouthful.

"Jeremy's got the first-day-back-after-vacation blues," Dad said.

"Where was Robbie this afternoon?" Mom asked. "You've been waiting for him to get back all week. I was sure you'd see him today."

"I think maybe he had to go clothes shopping," Jeremy told her. He didn't really think Robbie had gone shopping, but it was a safe bet this time of year.

"That's funny," Mom said. "Anne didn't say anything about that when I saw her."

Mom was good friends with Robbie's mother. They both worked at the mall and they saw a lot of each other.

"Dad, you should see the periscope Mr. Applebaum helped me make." Jeremy tried changing the subject. "It really works."

"Show it to me after dinner," Dad said. "Mr. Applebaum sure is clever for such a pack rat. I'll give him that."

Jeremy wished his dad wouldn't call Mr. Applebaum a pack rat. It sounded like Dad was making fun of his friend, and that made him feel bad.

"I really wish you wouldn't spend so much time over there," Mom started again. "You should be playing with children your own age. With all that junk, it isn't safe."

"The place looks like a natural disaster." Andrea had to add her two cents.

"It does not."

"It does, too," Andrea persisted. "I'm surprised someone doesn't report him."

"That's enough, you two," Dad said. "I think Jeremy is all right at Applebaum's. There's a lot worse he could get into. Why, I could tell you things we did when we were kids that would make your hair stand on end."

"Tell us," Andrea said. She and Jeremy both liked Dad's stories about when he was a boy. Jeremy especially liked the one about the tree fort Dad built and how once he slipped and fell, narrowly escaping death when he landed upside down on a bottom branch hanging by his knees.

"Oh, please, Nick." Mom groaned.

"Your mom's right," Dad said. He made shifty eyes. "The dinner table is no place for discussing such dastardly deeds. Your mother doesn't have the stomach for it."

Jeremy smiled.

"Besides, the sooner you kids get this table cleared, the sooner we can have dessert," Dad added.

Later that evening, Jeremy was doing his homework at the kitchen table. He had a desk in his room, but he liked being downstairs. Mom and Dad were in the living room, reading the paper. He could hear them talking every once in a while. The dishwasher made a quiet swooshing noise and the globe lamp over the table threw a circle of yellow light around him. Jeremy felt comfortable there, doing his spelling work. Mrs. Weaver always made them write out the whole page. It took forever.

Jeremy wrote the numbers one through twenty-five down the left-hand side of the paper. He put his name on the top right-hand side, and the date under it. Under that he put *Rm. 205.*

The hum of the dishwasher went off, and the kitchen was perfectly quiet. Jeremy had just finished the first section of spelling when he heard a tinkling noise. He stopped and listened, but the noise stopped. He began his work again and the noise started again. It seemed to be coming from the sink.

Jeremy got up and took a look. There was a spoon inside a glass lying down next to the opening to the garbage disposal. *Funny,* Jeremy thought, *the spoon must have jiggled against the glass. Maybe vibration from the dishwasher.* He rinsed out the glass with a splash of water from

14

the faucet, and helped himself to some milk from the fridge. Then he sat down again and took out a clean piece of paper.

He drew a long arm. It had two levers at one end and two pinchers at the other and a joint in the middle. *With a mechanical arm like that,* Jeremy thought, *while you were sitting at the table you could reach out and take a glass off the counter, put it on the table, and then reach around and open the fridge door. Then you could pick up the milk, bring it to the table, and pour it without even getting up.*

Jeremy liked to design inventions. Someday he was going to be famous like Einstein or the Wright brothers. He just needed to invent something that no one else had ever thought of.

Mom came into the kitchen and began making a cup of tea. "Mom," Jeremy said, "tell me some kind of invention you need to get stuff done around here. I need an invention to design."

"Let me see." Mom thought for a minute. "How about a machine to pick up those Legos all over your room, or one to sort all different toy pieces? I could have really used that when you were younger."

"Right," Jeremy said. "Now you've got *me* to do it. Come on, Mom. I need a real invention."

Mom poured a cup of tea. "I've got it," she said. "How about a laundry sorter and clothes folder?"

She stood behind Jeremy and looked over his shoulder. "Is this really for homework?"

"Not really," Jeremy mumbled. He pushed his drawings under the spelling book.

"Better get to work," Mom said as she took her tea back to the living room.

Jeremy leaned his head on his arm and started reading.

It was hard to concentrate. Jeremy felt as if someone were watching him. He knew no one was there, but he turned around to make sure. Something on the counter caught his eye. It was a gray flash, a shadow. Jeremy blinked. There was nothing there. He turned around again and tried to figure out the answer to number twenty-three.

A moment later he heard a rustling noise. This time he knew he had heard it. There it was again! A shiver ran down Jeremy's neck. He turned back toward the counter, very slowly this time, holding his breath.

Then Jeremy jumped. There, sitting on the counter, trying to get into the foil-covered brownie pan, was the cutest gray mouse. He sat up on his hind legs with his pinkish white tail wrapped in front, and stared at Jeremy. Then he was gone. He was so fast, he seemed to vanish into thin air.

Jeremy blinked. It was like a mirage. He hopped out of his chair and started moving the flour and sugar canisters where the mouse had been. *He must be behind here somewhere,* Jeremy thought, but nothing was there. Had Jeremy been seeing things? He sat down again to think about it.

Andrea came into the kitchen. "Hey, Squirt," she said.

"Don't call me Squirt," Jeremy said without even raising his head from his book. Jeremy was especially sensitive to that name because he was just about the shortest kid in the fifth grade. Even Melinda Belk was nearly as tall as him this year, and she was practically a midget.

"Listen," Andrea said. "Do you think Mr. Applebaum has any small weights over there in all that stuff?"

"Probably," Jeremy told her.

"Kim and I need them for our next science project. Can you get me some?"

"I'll try, if you quit calling me Squirt and stop talking about what a mess Mr. A.'s garage is," Jeremy told her.

"Great. Thanks." Andrea started to leave the kitchen.

"Andrea, guess what?" Jeremy intended to tell his sister about his visitor, but he remembered something. Andrea was always gassing butterflies and bugs and mounting them for science projects. She dissected a worm once, and last year she made Jeremy catch a frog for her in the old cemetery lily pond down the street. When Jeremy found out she was going to dissect the frog, he let the poor animal go.

"What do you want?" Andrea asked impatiently. "I have to finish my homework. I promised Jamie I'd call her tonight."

"Never mind," Jeremy told her.

"OK, Squirt. Don't forget my weights." Andrea ran out of the kitchen and pounded up the stairs.

"Cut that out," Jeremy objected halfheartedly. He wanted to finish his homework, but he had more exciting things to think about. He worked on the last two questions and waited for the mouse to come back. He thought about telling Mom and Dad, but he realized that might be dangerous for his mouse. Mom still had poison roach traps in the basement because once Jeremy had told her he had seen cockroaches in Mr. Applebaum's garage. She was afraid he was going to bring them into their house, and she had even made him stay home from the Applebaums' for a whole week.

No, better to keep this a secret. It could be like having a pet. Mom said pets were too much trouble, especially when you went away on vacation, and Dad agreed. So Jeremy didn't have any pets. But it looked like this mouse knew how to take care of himself. Jeremy wondered where his mouse lived and how often he came into the kitchen.

He was so fast, Jeremy thought, *it was like all I saw was his shadow. That's what I could name him. Shadow. Or Flash. That's it, Flash. I'll call him Flash. I have a pet mouse and his name is Flash.* Jeremy imagined telling the kids at school. He imagined telling Robbie.

"Jeremy," Dad called from the living room. "Time to get ready for bed."

It looked like Flash wasn't going to come back now. Jeremy decided to leave a treat for him. He got a piece of cheddar cheese from the refrigerator and put it behind the flour canister, where he hoped Mom wouldn't notice it.

I know I saw him, Jeremy told himself as he got ready for bed. *If the cheese is gone tomorrow, I'll know for sure.*

Chapter 3

There was one person at the bus stop before Jeremy on Tuesday. Jeremy knew it was Robbie even before he got to the corner. He and Robbie were the only two kids who got on at that stop.

"Hey, Jer, what's new?" Robbie walked over to meet Jeremy.

"Nothing," Jeremy said. Robbie was being real friendly, more like his usual self. "How was your visit with your dad?"

"Great," Robbie said. "We went to Great Gorge Amusement Park with my cousins. I even got to go on the Steel Demon. It was awesome."

"Wow," Jeremy said. Robbie always got to do

neat things at his dad's. For two summers Jeremy and Robbie had been planning to go to Scottsdale Amusement Park together. It was the biggest amusement park around, but it was in the next county. Dad said it was too far, and Robbie's mom said it was too expensive. "You're lucky," Jeremy told his friend.

He felt bad that Robbie had gotten to go to an amusement park that was even better than Scottsdale, but he was glad Robbie was acting more normal. Besides, Jeremy had something special to tell, too.

"Guess what?" he asked, and before Robbie could answer he went on, "I have a pet mouse. His name is Flash. He's the neatest gray mouse you ever saw. I wasn't sure last night, but I put a piece of cheese out and this morning it was gone. I checked before anyone else was up."

"Where'd you get him? I don't believe your mom let you." Robbie was interested. His mom wouldn't let him have pets, either. He and Jeremy sometimes went to the pet store up on Murray Avenue after school to look at the puppies. They picked out the ones they liked best and gave them names. "Do you have a cage?" Robbie asked. "And what do you mean, you weren't sure?"

"No, he doesn't live in a cage," Jeremy explained. "I don't know where he lives exactly.

Somewhere in our kitchen. I saw him last night, right up on the counter, staring at me when I was doing homework. He was trying to eat the brownies. No one else knows about him." Jeremy paused, then added, "So don't tell your mom, OK?"

"That's not a real pet," Robbie told him. "That's just like having rats or cockroaches or something. We had mice in our apartment once. My mom used sticky paper to catch them and then she drowned them."

Jeremy winced. *How could someone drown anything as cute as Flash?*

"Anyway," Robbie continued, "my dad got a dog, and he says she's mine whenever I'm there. She's a big German shepherd. Her name is Sue and I got to feed her all week so she knows I'm her master. She's a watchdog and we could train her to be an attack dog if we wanted to."

The bus pulled up. Jeremy silently followed Robbie on and sat down next to him. Robbie was quiet, too. Jeremy almost wished he hadn't told his friend about Flash. He should have kept it a secret all to himself. Robbie was trying to act like everything he did or had was better than anything of Jeremy's. He was probably going to tell his mom about Flash.

Jeremy felt a tug on his shirtsleeve. "Look," Robbie said. He slid a piece of paper out of his notebook, holding it behind the notebook cover so no one else could see it. Jeremy looked at the paper. It was a picture from a magazine. He took a sharp breath. It was a woman and all she had on was underwear, fancy black underwear.

Robbie took his pen out of his back pocket and drew two circles on the women's chest and snickered. Jeremy's face felt hot. He knew he was blushing. He bent his head down so no one would see and he wouldn't have to look at the picture.

"What's the matter?" Robbie asked. "Didn't you ever see one before? I got it from my cousin Cliff. He's in middle school."

"Sure," Jeremy told him, "I got a sister, you know." He hoped that would shut Robbie up. Jeremy was sick of hearing about Robbie's dad and his cousins.

"Yeah?" Robbie said. "So what's the matter? I got a whole magazine like this. Cliff has a pile of them. He keeps them under his bed and his mom doesn't even notice. I did a lot of stuff with Cliff all week."

"It's dumb," Jeremy said. He didn't really know what was the matter. He just didn't feel right looking at pictures like that. "Why do you have to act so tough all of a sudden?" Jeremy hissed at Robbie.

The bus stopped in front of the Manor Day School, and Jeremy and Robbie both stood up. Jeremy moved out into the aisle and Robbie nudged him as he shoved ahead, saying, "Chill out. You're too serious. I'm out of here." Robbie pushed his way down the aisle.

When Jeremy got off the bus, he saw Robbie up ahead with those sixth-graders from yesterday. They were looking at something in Robbie's notebook and laughing and making exaggerated faces. Jeremy knew what they were doing. A couple of other friends said hi, but Jeremy walked slowly toward the fifth-grade entrance by himself.

There were four fifth-grade classes at Manor Day. Jeremy and Robbie were in different homerooms, so they usually only saw each other in art, math, and gym, and on the playground at lunch. Today they sat at different lunch tables. Out on the playground they both played soccer, and Robbie acted like nothing had happened. He picked Jeremy for his team just like always. Jeremy usually got picked right away because even though he was short, he was fast. He liked dribbling the ball down the field. Sometimes he practiced at home and he felt like that ball was a part of him. Now he wove back and forth between players and kicked.

"That's a goal for us," Robbie shouted. "Way to go, Jer."

"Jeremy hogs the ball," Michael yelled.

"Oh, cut it out," Robbie told him. "Just because you can't score." The bell rang. "See you later," Robbie called to Jeremy.

24

"Sure," Jeremy said. He felt better than he had all morning.

When they got off the bus after school, Robbie said, "I can't come over today. I got stuff to do."

"Me, too," Jeremy told him. He walked the half block home by himself. He was glad Robbie hadn't come. He couldn't wait to check on Flash, and he didn't need any comments from his friend.

When Jeremy came around the corner of the house, Mom was already working in the garden. Good. No one was in the kitchen.

"Hey, Mom," Jeremy called, starting up the back steps.

"Wait a minute," Mom said. "Come tell me about school. Is Robbie coming over? You two boys should get off on your bikes in this beautiful weather."

There she goes again, Jeremy thought, *trying to keep me from going over to Mr. Applebaum's.*

"He's busy," Jeremy told her. To make her feel better, he added, "He might come over later."

"Did you boys have a fight or something?"

"Mo-ommm," Jeremy said. "No. Robbie just said he's got stuff to do. We played soccer at lunch and I was on Robbie's team."

"Well, I might have some chores for you to do. I need some help turning over this garden."

"Sure, Mom. Later, though." Jeremy headed back toward the kitchen door.

"Wait a minute," Mom said again. She stood

25

up, brushed the dirt off her pant legs, and pulled the shovel out of the dirt. "Look at the nice job your Mr. Applebaum did repairing our shovel handle. It's bound to last longer than I will." Then she looked toward the hedges and shook her head. "Look at that yard, though. It just gets worse and worse. More junk seems to pile up every day. It's a wonder that man can find anything over there. I'd be afraid to see inside the garage."

Jeremy followed his mother's gaze past the hedge. There were at least five long ladders leaning against one side of the garage. Some were wooden and some were metal. There was an old cable spool as big as a table, ten or more drain pipes lying all over, and a pile of other pipes and chains and old drain covers. There was even an old sink out there. That's where Jeremy had found the toilet seat and cover for his fort. Everything was kind of rusty, but Jeremy didn't think it looked so bad.

There was a big fan-shaped trellis against one side of Mr. Applebaum's garage with a rosebush climbing on it. The bush was just starting to turn green and sprout. Jeremy could smell the fragrant lilacs that were beginning to burst with purple at the corner of the garage.

"I was talking to Mr. Hull at the grocery store this morning," Mom said. "He's worried about all that junk. He's afraid one of his kids will wander

26

over there and get hurt. I was embarrassed to tell him you actually play there."

"It's none of his business," Jeremy mumbled. He knew who Mr. Hull was. He lived about four or five houses down the street on the left-hand side and had about seven kids, all still rug rats as far as Jeremy could tell.

"He's thinking about filing a complaint," Mom added.

"What do you mean?" Jeremy asked. "What kind of a complaint? With the police or something? Can he do that?"

"I suppose," Mom said. "If it becomes enough of a public nuisance."

"That's not fair," Jeremy said. "Mr. Applebaum hasn't done anything wrong. He's not a public nuisance. Those kids are a public nuisance, if you ask me." A bunch of them were always jumping out in front of Jeremy when he was on his skateboard, trying to make him fall off.

"Take it easy," Mom said. "Mr. Hull didn't say he was going to do anything. He just said he was concerned. But I guess he's not the only one."

Jeremy sighed and turned toward the house. First Robbie was giving him trouble, and now it looked like Mr. Applebaum had trouble he didn't even know about. Jeremy wondered if he should warn him.

Chapter 4

Jeremy checked in the kitchen for the toast he'd left Flash. He had put a quarter piece back between the flour and sugar canisters. Now he pulled each jar out from the wall to make sure the toast was gone.

Jeremy was satisfied. Flash really did live nearby. Last night he had eaten the cheese and now he had taken the toast.

Turning to get his own snack, Jeremy noticed something stuck in the iron grate over the front burner of the stove. It was the toast, most of the quarter piece he had left, resting partway down the hole where the gas and flame come out. It was a little broken or chewed around the edges, but Jeremy knew it was the same piece. So that's where Flash had gone, into the stove! He had tried to pull the toast in, but it was too big.

Jeremy tucked that piece of information away for future reference: small pieces of food for Flash. Then he grabbed the toast and tossed it into the trash under the sink just as Mom was coming in the back door.

After he changed, Jeremy headed next door, still thinking about Flash. He wondered if Flash had a nest somewhere in the stove or under it or behind it. That sounded dangerous, but he figured Flash knew what he was doing. It was fun having a secret pet. Jeremy wished he hadn't told Robbie about Flash. He just better not tell his mom, Jeremy thought.

As Jeremy walked up Applebaum's driveway, he decided that Mom sure was right about one thing. It seemed like Mr. A. got new stuff every day. Off to one side of the driveway, there was a pile of rotting firewood, an old rusty pump, and a weathered wagon wheel. There were some cans of paint piled up with the colors all dripped down the sides, hardened and peeling off. As far as Jeremy could remember, that had all been there before. But today there was also a pile, about three feet high, of some kind of metal frames. Each one had rows and rows of little wheels.

Jeremy looked at them more closely. They were sections, really—each one was about two feet by four feet with about ten rows of wheels across and thirty wheels in each row. He ran his hand over the wheels. Some kind of rollers to move things, that's what they were.

Mr. Applebaum came around the side of the garage whistling his usual tune, soft and sad. He smiled when he saw Jeremy.

"Sneaking up on me, were you, son?"

"No." Jeremy knew Mr. A. was teasing him. "What's this?" he asked, pointing to the pile of rollers.

"Those?" Mr. Applebaum said. "I got those from the old grocery store they're tearing down over on Wade Street. They're practically antique. Used to use 'em to move boxes and such."

"I thought it was something like that," Jeremy told him.

"I just bet you did, too. Pretty smart for your britches, aren't you?" Mr. Applebaum winked at Jeremy and disappeared into the garage. Jeremy followed him.

"I remember when they first built that old store." Mr. Applebaum went on. "Those conveyers were a new invention."

"What are you going to do with them?"

Mr. Applebaum shrugged. "Can't say I know. I'll just keep them for a spell, I expect."

Jeremy looked around the room. That's what he liked about Mr. Applebaum's garage. Every time he went in there he noticed something different or he saw things in a new way.

There was an old black wood-burning stove with the burners missing. Sometimes the chickens laid their eggs in there. There was a whole stack of wooden crates. Jeremy wanted to use a couple to build a go-cart. He just needed the right wheels. There was an old chipped ceramic basin full of corks. Jeremy wanted to make a model boat out of them with toothpicks, and he could use some of the wooden spools he had seen in the bucket in the corner. Ropes were coiled up everywhere, and there were all kinds of wire. Some of it was coated electrical wire that would be great for making little figures.

A long, narrow workbench ran the length of the back wall. Jeremy could distinguish parts of an old lamp there in the dim light, along with stacks of flat plastic circles. He didn't know what the circles were for, but he knew they made great little Frisbees. There was a lot of other stuff in Mr. Applebaum's garage that Jeremy couldn't figure out a name or a use for.

He remembered what his mom had said about Mr. Hull complaining.

"Ever think of fixing this place up?" he asked. "Cleaning it a little, I mean."

Mr. Applebaum chuckled. "Not half so much as some folks do." He shrugged one shoulder toward the open door. Outside, Jeremy could see Mrs. Applebaum out hanging wet tea towels on the clothesline. She was short and a little bent over. As he watched, she tossed one towel up to snag the line, then pulled it down so she could reach it to squeeze the pegs on.

Mr. Applebaum smiled at Jeremy. "That woman is always trying to get me to do something I don't have a mind to do. Get me a haircut, clean out the garage, haul some of this stuff away. Seems like it's best if I just hide out here."

"Yeah," Jeremy agreed.

"Now, why'd I haul it away if I just brought it here?" Mr. Applebaum continued.

Jeremy sympathized. "I know what you mean. Mom's always trying to get me to clean my room. Where do you get all this stuff, anyway?"

Mr. Applebaum was sorting through some piles of screws and nails. "Oh, here and there. Lots of it came from the old job."

Jeremy knew Mr. Applebaum used to be the foreman on a construction team.

"Rich, the new foreman over there, a nice young fellow, he calls me up now and then when they got something they got no use for and think I might like to have."

Jeremy looked at the rusty parts to an old-fashioned hand pump. He moved the arm up and down. It screeched and clanked. "Some of this stuff is pretty old," he observed.

"Been here near as long as I have," Mr. Applebaum confirmed. "Friends give it to me. I used to get things from the dump, but you can't do that nowadays. Still can get some things at the curbside on trash days."

"Yeah, I got a great dragon poster in the trash. I've got it hanging over the head of my bed." Jeremy had found it on the way to school and hidden it in the bushes so the trashman wouldn't get it. He had picked it up on the way home again. Mom wasn't too happy when he brought it into the house. She was worried about bugs and dirt and germs, but she finally let him keep it.

Mr. Applebaum chuckled. "I happen to know that some people dump stuff here. They got something they don't want anymore and don't know what else to do with. 'Got something you might like, Samuel,' they say. They just want to get rid of it." Mr. Applebaum shook his head and chuckled again. "Don't bother me none, though."

Jeremy nodded, but he felt a little uncomfortable. Now Mr. Applebaum's car not only didn't fit in the garage, but with those new rollers out there, he wasn't even going to have room to pull it up close to the entrance.

Jeremy went back outside and started piling

things up a little. He lifted a few paint cans up on top of one another and tried straightening some of the piles of bricks. Maybe he could at least make room for the car. He tried lifting the sections of rollers, but they were pretty heavy. All he succeeded in doing was moving the top section cockeyed so it didn't line up with the others. That just made it worse.

I could use some kind of crane, Jeremy thought. *A crane, or at least a lever and pulley. A wheel and axle, lever, pulley, inclined plane, screw, and wedge.* Those were the simple machines they were studying in science class. This job was going to take more than a simple machine, Jeremy thought. More like what Mom wanted for cleaning his room, only this job called for the super-duper durable deluxe model for garage and outdoor work.

Jeremy smiled to himself. It had a nice ring to it. Now if he could only invent it. Something like a vacuum cleaner that could suck up the small stuff, with a bulldozer on the front for the bigger stuff, and a crane off to the side. You would definitely need some kind of sorting mechanism, too.

"Want to give me a hand, son? Or would you rather stand round and moon all day?" Mr. Applebaum's voice broke into Jeremy's thoughts.

"Sure," Jeremy said. "I'll help."

He followed Mr. Applebaum back into the garage. *It's not so bad in here,* he thought. *If I stacked a few more things up, it would make room for some of the stuff outside.* Nobody could complain about what was inside the garage, Jeremy figured.

"Carry this out to the garden for me," Mr. Applebaum said. He held up a large sheet of glass for Jeremy to take. "Careful now, don't hurt yourself."

Mr. Applebaum took another sheet of glass in one hand and grabbed the shovel and a crinkled-up brown paper bag with the other.

There was an old pigeon coop built onto the back of the garage. The soft sound of the pigeons cooing reminded Jeremy of Mr. Applebaum's song.

He helped Mr. Applebaum dig two shallow holes. The brown paper bag had tiny lettuce seeds in it, and Mr. Applebaum showed Jeremy how to sprinkle them in neat even rows in the holes. Then Mr. Applebaum attached the hose to the spigot at the edge of the garden. He didn't have a nozzle, but he showed Jeremy how to hold his thumb over the stream of water at the end of the hose to make a light spray.

Jeremy marveled at the old man's big rough hands, weathered like the driftwood stacked at the back of the garage, with dirt in the cracks and under the fingernails. There was a stump on his left hand where his second finger should be. The first time Jeremy had realized his friend only had four fingers on one hand, he was shocked. Mr. Applebaum had told him about the time when he was a young man and used to do farm work. "I was repairing the tractor and the blame thing just started up and took my finger." Mr. Applebaum told Jeremy it had looked like rain, so he had to finish the haying before he went to the doctor. "Just wrapped a hanky around the whole mess and got the hay in with the first drop of rain. Doctor said I might have saved the finger if I'd come in sooner, but I told him I still got nine more fingers plus a barn full of hay." Now Jeremy hardly noticed the stump.

Jeremy helped put the glass plate over the two holes with the seeds. "Kind of a hothouse," Mr. Applebaum explained. "Keeps those rascal chipmunks away from the new leaves for a while, too." He stood up slowly. "Soon be time to get me some tomato seeds."

"Samuel, Samuel." Someone was calling and rattling the back gate at the far end of the garden. Jeremy and Mr. Applebaum both turned. Mrs. Sullivan was standing in her yard. She was wearing baggy pants and a gray kerchief tied under her chin. "Have you got my lamp fixed yet?" she called.

"Nope," Mr. Applebaum told her.

"Well, come here, young man," she said, shaking some hedge clippers toward Jeremy. "Take these shears to Samuel. See if he can get them sharpened on that old stone wheel of his."

Jeremy looked at his friend. "Go ahead," Mr. Applebaum said. Jeremy walked across the garden with clods of fresh dirt sticking to his sneakers as he moved. He took the clippers from Mrs. Sullivan.

She shook her head. "I'm surprised your mother lets you over there." She looked past Jeremy. "Look at those filthy birds. Right next to the garden, too. There ought to be a law against such things." She was talking loud enough for the whole neighborhood to hear. Jeremy was embarrassed for his friend. "I got to look at this mess every day." Mrs. Sullivan shook her head. "Unsightly," she murmured, "unsightly."

Jeremy walked back to Mr. Applebaum and handed him the clippers. "Did you hear what she said?"

"Ah, she don't mean no harm," Mr. A. said. But Jeremy wasn't so sure.

Chapter 5

On Wednesday, Jeremy didn't see much of Robbie in school. At lunch recess Robbie didn't play soccer. Jeremy could see him over at the edge of the playground with those other kids. The big one's name was Tom Morgan. Andrea went to school with his older brother, Pat. When Jeremy asked her if she knew him, she said Pat was always in trouble and had even been suspended once. He hadn't told her Robbie was hanging out with those kids.

Jeremy felt good running with the ball. He felt in control when he could dribble down the field, line up a shot, and shoot for a goal or an assist.

He and Robbie usually played well together. It seemed each of them always knew where the other would be, ready for a pass without even looking. Jeremy missed his friend, but he didn't want his bad feelings about Robbie getting in the way of his game. He was just as glad Robbie stayed away if he was going to hang around with Tom and that gang.

Coming home, Jeremy sat in the front of the bus. He didn't see Robbie, and when he got off, he didn't wait for him. Jeremy wanted to get home fast. If he got in before Mom, he could check up on Flash and get over to Mr. A.'s in time to clean things up a little and still do some work on the fort.

Jeremy put his backpack on the counter. The bananas in the fruit bowl were just the way he liked them, still all yellow and just a little soft. As he yanked at the biggest one he noticed something strange about the half banana left from breakfast. It was still attached to the bunch, and the end where Andrea had sliced it was turning brown. What was interesting was that it wasn't flat across the cut end anymore. The end of the banana had been dug out, and Jeremy could almost see the tiny teeth marks. He knew right away that Flash had had a good meal. He could just picture him in the fruit bowl nibbling away.

Jeremy took a steak knife from the drawer and

cut the end off the half banana to destroy the evidence. Mom was due home any minute, and it would look suspicious if he left the half-eaten part near the stove for Flash. He tossed it in the trash, grabbed his own banana, and headed upstairs to change.

On his way back down Jeremy thought about how fast he got home when he wasn't messing around with Robbie. If Mom didn't stay at work late or stop to do an errand, she almost always got in just before him. Today he was home and changed, and she hadn't even arrived yet. It was a good thing, because otherwise, she would have seen the teeth marks in the banana.

Jeremy turned the corner into the kitchen and jumped. There was Flash, sitting right up on the counter staring at him. Jeremy figured he had startled the mouse even more than Flash had startled him. He could imagine the tiny little heart beating like crazy, the mouse hoping Jeremy hadn't seen him.

Jeremy stood perfectly still and waited. Then suddenly Flash was gone again behind the canisters.

Slowly, Jeremy moved each canister out so he wouldn't scare the mouse. Jeremy knew he hadn't made it to the stove, and there was nowhere else he could go. He was sure to find him this time. But there was nothing there. The rascal had disappeared again. Back behind the stove this time, Jeremy figured. There was a little space between the stove and the wall. That was the only explanation. Jeremy replaced the canisters just as Mom opened the back door.

"Robbie's on his way over here to ride bikes," she told him. "I passed him on his bike on my way home."

"Are you sure he was coming here?" Jeremy asked. He really didn't feel like riding bikes today. He had other plans.

"Where else would he be going? Anne said she was going to send him over today so you two could get some fresh air."

So that was it. Mom and Robbie's mom had planned this. Sure enough, there was Robbie. Jeremy saw the top of his red brown head glide past the kitchen window. In a minute Robbie was at the door. "Hi, Mrs. Blake. Hi, Jer."

"Hello, Robbie," Mom said. "It's good to see you. How was your vacation?"

"Great," he said, and turned to Jeremy. "Want to ride bikes?"

Jeremy figured he didn't have much choice. Mom was right there. What could he say?

"OK," he answered. "For a little while."

"You boys take a nice long ride. Get some exercise," Mom called after them as they went down the back steps.

Jeremy wheeled his bike out of the garage. Robbie walked alongside him. "My mom's making me do this," Robbie said.

"Yeah," Jeremy said. He'd figured that.

"So where do you want to go?"

"I don't know."

"What about the fort?" Robbie asked.

"Nah," Jeremy said. "Let's ride." No way he was going to take Robbie over to Mr. A.'s after that crack about forts being for babies.

"OK. How about the candy store?"

"I need to get my money," Jeremy said.

"Don't worry about it," Robbie told him as he hopped on his bike. "Come on."

Jeremy rode up next to Robbie. "Since when do you treat?" Jeremy teased Robbie. "Got a job or something?" They always joked about never having any spending money. Neither Jeremy nor Robbie was allowed to have a paper route. Mom said she'd end up doing all the work, and Mrs. Fuller said the same thing. Both boys got an allowance, but Robbie had to put half of his in the bank every week, so Jeremy was always treating him or giving him a loan. Robbie was going to pay him back when he turned eighteen. If Robbie was going to treat, maybe he really wanted to be friends again.

"Something like that," Robbie said as he sped ahead of Jeremy.

Jeremy felt great coasting down the hill. Mom was right. He hadn't been on his bike for a long time. The fresh spring air felt good as it raced past him, and the sun was warm. This wasn't such a bad idea after all.

The candy store was really the neighborhood pharmacy on Main Street across from the Town Hall. Mr. Dickson still sold old-fashioned penny candy, and a lot of that was five and ten cents apiece, but Jeremy preferred Milky Ways and Snickers bars and M&M's. They were the most expensive ones.

Mr. Dickson was in the pharmacy at the back of the store when the boys went in. Jeremy followed Robbie to the candy bars.

"What kind do you want?" Robbie whispered.

"Milky Way," Jeremy said, then changed his mind as Robbie reached for the Milky Way. "No, maybe M and M's."

"Make up your mind," Robbie hissed. He picked up a bag of M&M's and a Milky Way bar. Then he turned around as if he were checking out the comic books across the aisle and looked sideways back toward Mr. Dickson. Then Robbie grabbed Jeremy's arm and said, "OK, let's go." He nudged Jeremy along in front of him up to the door.

"Hey, wait," Jeremy said. "You forgot to—"

"Shh." Robbie glared at him. "Let's go."

"What's the matter?" Jeremy asked when they got outside. "Aren't you going to buy the candy?"

"Come on," Robbie said as he hopped on his bike.

Jeremy followed him down the block. Robbie stopped at the corner and propped one foot on the curb. "Here," he said, grinning, as he tossed Jeremy the M&M's. He took a Milky Way bar out of his pocket, too.

"But you didn't pay," Jeremy said, looking back over his shoulder.

"Right," Robbie said smugly. "I told you money wasn't a problem. Cliff showed me how. It's easy. Boy, Mr. Dickson is dumb. I didn't even need you to cause a distraction or anything."

"But that's stealing," Jeremy protested.

"It's called shoplifting," Robbie corrected him. "No one will ever know. He's not going to miss a few candy bars."

Jeremy felt sick to his stomach. He looked back toward the pharmacy. He expected the police to drive up any minute. "We could get into real trouble," he told Robbie.

"Relax," Robbie said. "I've done it before."

Jeremy didn't want to hear about it. He knew he should go back and give Mr. Dickson the M&M's, but he didn't have the money to pay for them, and how was he going to explain where he got them? He could put them back on the shelf, but what if Mr. Dickson saw him?

44

Jeremy just wanted to get away from Robbie and far away from the pharmacy. *Why'd Robbie have to do it? Why'd he have to do it in front of me?* Jeremy threw the M&M's back at Robbie and took off at top speed. He felt disgusted and dirty, and he wanted to wipe the whole memory out of his brain, like it never happened. He pedaled as fast as he could, and he hoped Robbie wasn't following him.

Chapter 6

Instead of hopping off his bike in the driveway, Jeremy pedaled right into the garage. He stayed in there for a few minutes trying to decide what to do. If Mom knew he was home, she would want to know why he had come back so soon, and Jeremy knew he couldn't tell her the truth.

If he could get to Applebaum's without her seeing him, he realized he could hang out over there until dinnertime. Why hadn't he ridden straight there in the first place? Jeremy poked his head out of the garage and scanned the yard and the kitchen window. The coast was clear. Feeling like a criminal, Jeremy darted out of the garage and squeezed through the hedges.

Mr. Applebaum was out in the garden. "Looks like we're finally going to get some rain," he greeted Jeremy. "We need it awful bad for the garden."

"How do you know it's going to rain?" Jeremy asked. He was relieved to have something safe and normal to talk about. As far as he could see, it was just as sunny and warm as it had been all week.

Mr. Applebaum pointed up to the top of the garage, where a weather vane perched on top of a cupola. "When that dog turns directly around in the opposite direction like it just done, we're bound to have rain by nightfall," he explained.

Jeremy gazed up at the silhouetted figure of a hunting dog stretched out across the arrow of the weather vane. It was poised in the point position with a front paw lifted up, tail straight out in one direction and nose in the other.

Jeremy knew Mr. Applebaum used to raise and train hunting dogs for shows. He had seen all the first-place blue ribbons his friend's dogs had won. They were in a glass case in his garage.

Mr. Applebaum knew everything, Jeremy thought, even how to predict the weather.

He watched as the broad-shouldered man bent over the humped rows where he had already planted seeds. Every now and then he stooped to pull a small weed. The strawberry leaves were greening up, and already there were a few tiny white flowers here and there. Jeremy couldn't wait. Mr. Applebaum grew the best and the sweetest strawberries around. Even Andrea agreed about that. Which reminded Jeremy of something.

"Hey, Mr. A., you got any weights in your garage?"

Mr. Applebaum stood up straight and thought for a minute. "Well, I did have a set of barbells somewhere in there. You thinkin' of building some muscles?"

"No," Jeremy said. "These are for my sister, Andrea. She needs them for a science project. I think she needs little ones."

The idea of lifting weights did intrigue Jeremy. Maybe a few muscles would make him look bigger, taller. He'd have to look around the garage for the barbells later.

"We can try the fishing-tackle box soon as I finish here," Mr. A. told him. "I used to have a whole boxful of sinkers."

"That sounds right." Jeremy followed his friend up and down the rows. He knew he should be working on his fort or trying to clean up that garage, but he didn't feel like it. He put his hands in his pockets and watched as Mr. Applebaum carefully studied each new sprout, breaking up a lump of dirt here and there and tossing a stone now and then. "Got to watch out for those rascal chipmunks," Mr. Applebaum observed. "I'll soon be setting me some traps."

"Traps?" Jeremy asked. "You're going to trap chipmunks?"

"Trap 'em and let them go in the woods over at the edge of the big cemetery."

Jeremy was relieved. He didn't think Mr. Applebaum would kill a chipmunk. Chipmunks were just as cute as mice. He wondered if you could keep one for a pet.

That made Jeremy think of Flash. He should have checked the kitchen to make sure Flash hadn't left any traces that his mom or Andrea could find. Flash had been right up on the counter just before Mom and Robbie had arrived. Maybe he would come out and Mom would see him. She would probably put rat poison out, or something. Jeremy felt like he needed to get home and protect Flash right away. But he couldn't go home yet because Mom would want to know where Robbie was and why Jeremy had come home so early.

Jeremy sighed. He felt like he had too many secrets. He couldn't talk to Robbie anymore. He had already told him too much about the fort and about Flash. Robbie was a thief, and he could never trust Robbie again.

"Hey, son." Mr. Applebaum spoke softly.

"Awful quiet, aren't you? Acting like you lost your best friend."

That startled Jeremy. How did Mr. Applebaum know? "No," he mumbled. Anyway, that was just a saying. Mr. Applebaum didn't know anything about Robbie and Jeremy couldn't tell him, anymore than he could tell his mom.

There *was* something Jeremy could talk to Mr. Applebaum about. "We have a mouse in our house," he blurted out. "It's gray with big ears and a pink tail."

"That's just a little house mouse," Mr. Applebaum told him. "They don't do no harm." He laughed a short deep ha-ha kind of laugh. "Bet your momma don't like it none, though." His eyes twinkled with the joke.

"She doesn't know about it," Jeremy said. "I found him. He lives behind the stove or inside somewhere and I feed him. His name is Flash."

"Flash, huh? That's a name for a mouse. Speedy little critter, is he?"

Jeremy nodded.

"Well," Mr. Applebaum said, "your momma won't want him chewing on the wires and all in her kitchen, I expect."

"No," Jeremy agreed. He hadn't thought about that.

"Now what do you feed this mouse of yours?" Jeremy told him about the cheese and toast and banana. "Try some peanut butter," Mr. Applebaum said.

"That's a great idea." Jeremy was glad he could tell someone about his mouse, someone who appreciated what it was like to have a secret pet.

Jeremy stayed at Applebaum's until he figured it was safe to go home. He wanted to check on Flash and, if he got a chance, try the peanut butter. Before he left, Mr. Applebaum let him pick some weights out of the tackle box for Andrea. He put them in his pocket.

Mom was in the kitchen preparing dinner. Spaghetti. It smelled great.

"How was the bike ride?" Mom asked.

"Fine," Jeremy lied.

"Where'd you go?"

Jeremy winced. "All around." He could never tell her they had been to the candy store. He didn't want to be associated with the scene of the crime.

Anyway, Mom had other things on her mind. "I'm running a little late," she said. "Think you could set the table for me?"

"Sure." Jeremy was happy to have her off the subject.

He pulled open the silverware drawer and started to count out four of everything when suddenly he noticed something. Little specks. Black specks. Jeremy looked closely. It couldn't be, but he knew it was. Mouse droppings. Boy, was Flash going to get into trouble! This was all Mom had to see. She'd have the rat poison out in no time.

Jeremy glanced at Mom. She was at the stove with her back to him. He needed to clean it up fast, but what could he use? Not the dishcloth. He needed something he could throw away. The paper towels were on the other side of Mom, and if he took one, she'd ask him what it was for. Mom always said that paper towels disappeared overnight in their house. Jeremy reached over and grabbed a paper napkin off the table.

"I have to go to a class tonight so I won't be home." Mom was talking as she stirred the sauce.

"No problem," Jeremy told her as he picked up the droppings with the napkin.

"What's no problem?" Andrea asked as she came into the kitchen.

Then before anyone could answer she exclaimed, "Oh, gross. That's disgusting." She was leaning over Jeremy's shoulder now.

Jeremy slammed the silverware drawer shut. How could she have seen? "What's your problem?" Jeremy asked, turning around to face his sister.

"Don't you ever wash your hands?" she retorted. "They're filthy."

After a moment of confusion, Jeremy felt sheer relief. Flash was safe for a little longer. He looked at his hands. They weren't so bad. "My hands aren't dirty," he told Andrea.

"Mom," Andrea demanded, "how could you let him set the table with hands like that? He's been playing over at that filthy garage."

How did Andrea know he'd been at Mr. Applebaum's? It was none of her business, but Jeremy couldn't afford to argue. He just wanted Andrea to go away. He still had to check the rest of the drawers.

He slammed the silverware down on the table and went to the sink. "I got your weights," he hissed at Andrea, "but don't bug me or I won't give them to you."

"Great, where are they?"

Jeremy reached into his pocket and handed her the weights. "Thanks," she said. "These are perfect."

"Now," Jeremy went on, "do you want to set the table or are you going to let me finish?"

"No problem," Andrea said, making for the stairs.

Jeremy made a quick check in the rest of the drawers. "Looking for something?" Mom questioned absently.

"I've got it," Jeremy assured her. Everything looked OK, for now, but he was going to have to make sure he cleaned up after Flash every day. He'd have to check every morning and afternoon.

That night, Jeremy couldn't sleep. Mom was still out at her quilting class with Robbie's mom. Maybe they would talk. He knew Robbie wouldn't tell his mom about the candy store, but maybe he'd gone straight home and Mrs. Fuller would mention that he got home early. Jeremy tried to push the whole thing out of his mind. *Just pretend it didn't happen,* he told himself. He could just stay away from Robbie, and no one would ever know.

Jeremy decided to think about Flash instead. He planned how he could put some peanut butter on toast for him. A light spring rain began to patter on the roof and Jeremy pulled the sheet up around his shoulders. Mr. Applebaum was right about the rain. Jeremy was very close to sleep. He woke again, for a moment remembering Mr. A. and how he had still not cleaned his garage. *Tomorrow,* Jeremy thought, and he was asleep.

Chapter 7

Jeremy was up early on Saturday morning. The rain had stopped and the sun was already beginning to push back the clouds, promising a fresh clear day. He got dressed quickly and crept downstairs even before Dad was up.

He went straight to the kitchen and made a quick but thorough check for any evidence that would give Flash away. He looked in all the drawers and then at the fruit bowl, but there was nothing to indicate that a small furry creature shared their home.

Jeremy was satisfied. He poured himself a big bowl of cornflakes and sliced a banana into it. Before he poured the milk he took one of the slices, spread a dab of peanut butter on it, and put it near the hole in the front burner of the stove.

Jeremy liked being the only one up in a sleeping house. It made him happy to think what a special breakfast Flash would have. Even the episode with Robbie yesterday didn't seem so bad. He could almost pretend it had never happened.

He was absentmindedly reading the cornflakes box as he ate when he heard a rustling noise behind him. It was Flash for sure. Jeremy kept himself from turning around so his friend wouldn't be scared away before he got to enjoy his treat. He stopped eating and waited, concentrating on being quiet and still until he couldn't stand it any longer. He turned very slowly until Flash was right there in his full view, working on the banana, his little nose and whiskers bobbing with each nibble. Suddenly Flash started. He stopped eating and perched rigid on the edge of the burner. Jeremy was slower to notice what Flash must have already sensed, a soft step on the stairs. Quickly, Jeremy jumped up and Flash disappeared through the burner. Jeremy whisked the half-eaten banana slice into the trash and covered it with a crumpled paper napkin. He was back in his seat when Andrea came into the room. She looked up at Jeremy and jumped, letting out a little yelp. Jeremy choked back a laugh.

"You startled me," Andrea said accusingly. "What are you doing here, anyway? I thought I was the only one up."

"Eating breakfast. What are you doing?"

Andrea grabbed an orange and a banana from the fruit bowl. "I'm going over to Kim's to work on our science project, early, so we can have the rest of the day to go to the mall. We're getting doughnuts for breakfast. Tell Mom I'll be home for dinner," she added as she went out the back door.

"Sure," Jeremy told his sister. Andrea was OK when she was in a good mood. Even so, it had been a close call. Jeremy knew it was only a matter of time before someone in his family found out about Flash. He cleaned up the crumbs and put his dishes in the sink. Then he made another check for evidence of Flash. There was nothing. "Sorry I can't leave you any treats now, Flash," he said out loud. "It's too risky. I got to go help Mr. Applebaum clean up his garage. He's the one who told me you would like peanut butter. See ya later," he called down the hole in the burner.

Jeremy found his friend unloading a whole pile of pipes from his station wagon. Pipes were piled up in the driveway in front of the rollers and the paint cans.

"Give me a hand, son," Mr. Applebaum said.

"Sure," Jeremy said. He helped guide one very

long thin pipe out of the back of the station wagon and found a place for it in the pile.

"Want me to bring these into the garage with those other pipes?" he asked. *At least that would neaten things up some,* Jeremy thought, *and get them out of the driveway.*

"No need," Mr. Applebaum told him.

"It's no problem," Jeremy insisted as he dragged two pipes toward the door. When he came back for two more pipes, he looked at the pile. There had to be fifty pipes there. Some of them were real long and skinny. Others were short and some were curved or bent. One had an S curve in it. That gave Jeremy an idea.

He went into the garage and brought out a wooden box full of old marbles. They weren't like the marbles Jeremy was used to. They were solid colors and most of them were opaque. Some of them were real old.

Jeremy propped a straight pipe up against the pile of rollers. He connected a Y-shaped pipe to the bottom. On one side of the Y he added the S curve, on the other side he added a straight pipe. Then he dropped a marble into the top. The marble came out the straight end.

Jeremy wondered how he could get it to come out the S-curve side. He propped the pipe up at a steeper angle and tried again. Jeremy dropped in several marbles at once. Then he tried racing one against another. The marbles made a whirring noise when they went through the pipes.

Jeremy had another idea. He went around the side of the garage and got the hose, which was still connected to the spigot. He stretched it back around the garage to the driveway. It just reached. Jeremy lined the hose up with the end pipe at the top. He ran back to the spigot and turned the water on. Then he raced back to the pipes and waited. In a second, the water rushed out of the pipes. He added some more pipes at the joints and made the water go in three different directions at once. It was like a whole plumbing system.

Jeremy wondered if he could pipe water into his fort. Mr. Applebaum had lots of old faucets lying around.

"Hey, Jer. That's neat." Jeremy looked up and saw Robbie standing over him. He had his bike. Behind him at the end of the driveway were the two sixth-graders, Tom and his friend.

"Yeah," Jeremy agreed. He put his head down and continued unscrewing the pipe he was working on. He wished Robbie would go away. "I have to turn the water off," he said, jumping up and heading toward the spigot. The water had made a river down the driveway and was running out into the street.

Jeremy stayed out by the spigot for a few minutes, hoping Robbie and his friends would leave, but they didn't. He went back and started unscrewing all the pipes.

Robbie was leaning on his handlebars. "So where's the fort?" he asked.

"Never mind," Jeremy mumbled. "What did you have to bring them for?"

"Come on, Robbie. This is kid stuff. Are you coming or not?" Tom called before Robbie could answer.

"Sure," Robbie called back. "This is no fun." He backed his bike around and pedaled off to meet his friends.

Good riddance, Jeremy thought as he headed back around the garage.

Mr. Applebaum was in the garden and Mr. Abbottello was talking to him over the side fence. "Sam, have you got any of those tomato seeds from last year?"

"Sure, I got some back in the garage. Got my seeds in already," he told his neighbor.

"I see that," Mr. Abbottello said. "They're looking fine. Wish I could say the same for that trash heap in your driveway, though."

"It don't hurt nothing."

"Maybe so," Mr. Abbottello said, rubbing his gray beard and gazing over at the driveway. "Think maybe I could use one of those bags of cement you got there? I got to mend my front step before the mailman falls and sues me."

"Help yourself," Mr. Applebaum told him. He turned back to look at his own garden and spoke to Jeremy. "What do you say we fill in that hole you got there to make some more room for my squash?"

"You mean the fort?" Jeremy asked. "Do we have to? I didn't even finish it yet."

Mr. Applebaum laughed. "Well, now, I thought you were tired of it. But I guess we got to let you finish it." He winked at Jeremy. "My boss lady tells me I've got too much planted for the two of us anyway." Jeremy knew Mr. Applebaum was talking about his wife, and he laughed, too. Mr. Applebaum usually supplied the whole neighborhood with vegetables all summer.

Jeremy spent the rest of the morning working on his fort. He was glad Robbie never came back.

"Sam-uuuu-elllll. Sam-uuuu-elllll! You come get this soup before it gets cold. Hear me?"

Jeremy poked his head up through the pink toilet seat cover. He saw Mr. Applebaum head for the back porch, where he stopped to remove his mud-caked shoes and rubbers. Nobody else Jeremy knew wore rubbers, but Mr. Applebaum always wore them over his old brown leather shoes. They were big and wide and curled up slightly at the toes. Jeremy thought they were like big old worn tires. Mr. Applebaum always slipped his rubbers off with the shoes still inside them.

Jeremy decided it was time for his lunch, too.

On the other side of the hedge he found his father under the hood of their Ford. Dad's hands were black with grease, and he had a pile of little nuts and bolts and things resting on the fender.

Jeremy peered over Dad's shoulder. "What's the problem?"

"Nothing major," Dad said. "Just a slow leak. I think this gasket is shot. I wonder if your Mr. Applebaum has got one that would fit."

"Maybe," Jeremy said. "He's eating lunch now."

"Sounds like a good idea," Dad said. "Think I'll get cleaned up and grab a bite, and then maybe see if he can help me after lunch. Seems like I've got a few extra pieces here," he added, looking puzzled.

"What's for lunch?" Jeremy asked Mom, taking a quick look around the kitchen for signs of Flash. There didn't seem to be any. He noticed a cut-off half banana in the fruit bowl. He peeled it and ate it so Flash couldn't leave any more telltale teeth marks.

"Soup, peanut butter, bologna," Mom said. "Help yourself, and clean up the mess."

"I always do," Jeremy teased.

Mom just said, "Humph."

Peanut butter was the easiest. He spread a gob on a piece of bread and then put on heaps of jelly so it wouldn't be too dry. He ate standing at the counter so he had only one messy place to clean up.

"By the way." Mom came back into the kitchen. "Anne called a few minutes ago. She's stuck and can't get out to the grocery store. She only needs a few things, and she was hoping you would go with Robbie on your bikes. She'll give you money for a pop."

The peanut butter stuck in Jeremy's throat even with all the jelly. He swallowed hard and took a drink of milk.

"I can't go," he told his mom.

"Jeremy, it won't take very long. I'm sure you can spare a few minutes. You'd better change your shirt first."

Jeremy thought he was going to have to tell Mom. She'd never make him go if she knew Robbie shoplifted. But he couldn't tell her. She'd be sure to tell Robbie's mom. He couldn't go, either. He didn't even want to see Robbie, let alone go shopping with him. Who knew what he might try to steal?

"Mom, I said I can't go."

"But I already told Anne you would."

"Well, you shouldn't have," Jeremy said sharply. "I—I don't feel good," he added more quietly.

Jeremy looked at the half-eaten sandwich in his hand. He really didn't feel good. He put the sandwich down on the counter and walked out of the room, then ran upstairs. Jeremy closed his bedroom door after him. He flopped on his bed, face first, and put the pillow over his head. Now Mom was really going to ask questions.

Chapter 8

"Jeremy, Jeremy, wake up. Jeremy, it's nearly time for dinner." Someone was shaking him. Jeremy shook off the sleep and tried to remember where he was. The pillow was lifted off his head. Jeremy rolled over and blinked. It was Mom. He had a bad taste in his mouth and his tongue felt furry.

Mom put a cool hand on his forehead and smoothed back his hair. "I'm sorry I made plans for you and Robbie without asking you first. It was my fault and I apologize. You really must not have been feeling well. You've slept nearly the whole afternoon."

It took a minute for Jeremy to focus on what

she was saying. Then he remembered, and a bad feeling crept over him. "What about the grocery store?" he asked.

"I phoned Anne and she said some other friends of Robbie's had stopped by and they could go with him. Anyway, I wanted you to know it's all right. I understand, and I'll try not to make plans for you again without checking with you first. Now, go wash your face and wake yourself up for dinner. I'm going to finish up in the kitchen. Dad and I are going out to the movies, so we want to eat early."

Jeremy absently rubbed the moist spot on his cheek where Mom had kissed him. Mom was great. She hadn't yelled at him at all. But she didn't understand anything. He stretched and rolled off the bed to a standing position. So Robbie went to the store with Tom and his friend. Jeremy was twice as glad he hadn't gone. In the bathroom, he splashed cold water on his face and began to feel human again.

Downstairs, in the kitchen, Jeremy made a quick check around for signs of his pet. There weren't any bananas in the fruit bowl, but Jeremy checked anyway and sure enough, there were more mouse droppings there. This was never going to work. Mom was sure to find some soon, and she would go through the ceiling. It would be all over for Flash.

Jeremy grabbed a paper napkin off the table

and quickly cleaned up the tiny bits of evidence. Would it be possible to house train a mouse, get him to go on a piece of paper towel or something? How was he going to do that if he hardly even saw Flash?

Maybe if he didn't have to worry about Mom or Andrea finding out, he could tame Flash, even teach him to do tricks. They had learned a little about conditioning in school. All he'd have to do is give Flash some peanut butter or banana when he did whatever he was supposed to do. He could build a maze for Flash, like the maze for marbles he had made out of the pipes at Mr. Applebaum's today.

"Jeremy? Are you still asleep?" Mom turned from the stove. "I've been talking to you and you haven't heard a word I said."

"Still waking up, I guess," Jeremy mumbled.

"Well, I said, do you know these boys Robbie was with today? Anne says she doesn't know them and she doesn't really like Robbie hanging around with older kids. I told her sixth grade wasn't that much older."

"I don't know them very well," Jeremy told her. It was true, but he had that uncomfortable feeling again, like he should tell her more.

*

"Hey, how come I didn't get a napkin?" Andrea asked as the family sat down to dinner.

"That's strange," Mom said. "I know I used the last one, but I was sure I had just enough when I set the table. I know I put four out." She glanced under the table and shook her own napkin to see if she had two. Then she reached across to check Jeremy's.

"Uh—I used yours," Jeremy stammered. "I, uh, needed to blow my nose."

"Oh, gross," Andrea commented.

"Here, take mine," Jeremy told his sister. "You need it more than I do."

"Thanks," Andrea said grudgingly. "But how do I know where it's been?"

"Well," Dad said, before Jeremy could answer, "the car is back to normal. Mr. Applebaum had the exact gasket I needed. That guy has got everything over there. Do you know, he's even got parts from an old Model T? Some of that stuff's probably worth something."

"Who'd want it?" Andrea groaned.

"You wanted his weights, all right," Jeremy pointed out.

"That's different."

"He should get rid of that stuff," Mom put in. "He can't possibly use it all."

"He's sure done a lot with his garden," Dad continued. "He showed me his tomato plants already sprouting, and that little greenhouse system he's got worked out."

"I can't wait for the corn," Andrea said.

"Those tomatoes are like nothing else I ever tasted," Mom said. "I just can't understand why my garden never produces anything like Mr. Applebaum's, even when I use his seeds."

Jeremy smiled. "Mr. A. says it's because of the pigeon fertilizer."

Andrea put her fork down. "Why don't you just keep Mr. Applebaum's secrets to yourself instead of spoiling my dinner?"

Jeremy was tired of having secrets, but he didn't say so.

"How's the science project coming, Andrea?" Dad asked.

"Great. It's due next week, and then we get to start a unit on anatomy. Everyone gets their own worm to dissect, and then each lab group gets a frog to do. My group already decided I can be the one to actually work on the frog, since I'm the one who wants to go to medical school."

Jeremy cringed. This was just what he'd been afraid of. Now Andrea would want to take a knife to any poor defenseless creature she could get her hands on in the name of medical science.

"Seems to me one of you kids already tried to dissect a worm when you were quite young. With your teeth. Was that you, Andrea?" Dad joked.

"Daaad," Andrea objected. "Please."

Jeremy had to smile, but he hated to think

about what would happen if Andrea found out about Flash.

"OK, you two," Mom said as she and Dad were getting ready to leave. "There's ice cream in the freezer and oatmeal cookies in the cookie jar. Help yourself, within reason. I picked up a couple of videotapes if you want to watch them. They're on top of the TV. Try to keep the arguing to a dull roar."

Andrea threw her arm across Jeremy's shoulder. "No problem. My little brother always behaves when I'm baby-sitting. Or I just lock the squirt in the closet."

"You aren't the baby-sitter," Jeremy objected.

"OK, kids, have a good evening," Dad said, holding the door for Mom.

"Bye," Jeremy said as he watched his parents leave. "Have a good time."

He walked back into the kitchen to get some dessert. Andrea was already on the phone in the hall closet. Jeremy could hear her giggle every now and then. He reached into the cookie jar and took an oatmeal cookie. Not exactly his favorite. Mom had put raisins in them again. Jeremy bit out the raisins on the outside and just ate around the ones in the middle. He threw the raisins in the trash and reached for another cookie. There wasn't much cookie left by the time you took all the raisins out. He took another bite and spit another raisin into his hand.

Then he had an idea. Raisins would be perfect mouse food. He collected a few more and put them on the stove. Mom and Dad wouldn't be home for hours, and Andrea would probably stay in the closet all night.

Jeremy got a bowl of ice cream and sat at the table. While he ate, he stared at the raisins so he could see Flash come out of his hole this time. Nothing happened, and he helped himself to a second bowl.

By the time he had finished, Flash still hadn't appeared and Jeremy was getting bored. *A watched mouse never pops up,* he told himself, laughing, as he rinsed the bowl. He left it in the sink and went into the living room to see what movies Mom had picked out. He hid the love story under the couch cushion and popped *The Hobbit* into the VCR. Then he stretched out on the couch with the purple-and-beige afghan over him. Maybe later he could get Andrea to make some popcorn. Jeremy could do it himself, but he figured it was worth a try to see if Andrea would do it. Flash would probably love some, too.

Thinking about popcorn made Jeremy thirsty. He jumped back off the couch and pressed *pause,* then dashed to the kitchen for a can of soda. Andrea was still on the phone. He remembered to check the raisins, but they were still there. There wasn't any soda, so Jeremy poured a glass of milk and added four heaping teaspoons of chocolate powder, twice the amount in the directions. Then he tossed the spoon in the sink and went back to the living room.

It was impossible to lean back on the couch and drink from the glass. Jeremy sighed. Maybe he could invent a table with an arm that swung out and around so he could rest his glass on it and sip the milk. Jeremy propped himself up with more pillows as the movie started.

"Help, Jeremy, Jerrrr-am-yyyy!" Andrea was shrieking. Jeremy jumped off the couch and met her in the hall.

"I just got off the phone and I was getting my cookies when I thought I heard something on the counter," she gabbled. "I thought I was hearing things but it happened again, and when I turned around, guess what?"

Jeremy knew, but he didn't say anything. Andrea didn't give him a chance anyway. "It was a mouse!" she exclaimed.

Jeremy walked over to the counter and took a close look, pushing the canisters around. He scooped the raisins off the stove into one hand. He was happy to see some were missing. "There's no mouse here."

"Of course not," Andrea told him in her big-sister tone, under control again. "It dashed away as soon as it saw me. It moved so fast I barely got a look at it. It was more like an impression."

"Is that what you were afraid of, an impression?" Jeremy said, sneering a little. Maybe he could talk Andrea out of thinking she had actually seen a mouse. "An impression of a mouse?"

Andrea put her hands on her hips. "It startled me, that's all."

Jeremy knew the feeling. He looked all around and even in the sink again. "What did the impression look like?"

"I don't know," Andrea said impatiently. "It went too fast. I barely saw anything but the movement. That's what startled me."

"Then how do you know it wasn't a rat or a snake or just your imagination?"

"It was a mouse," Andrea insisted. "My brain can assimilate that even if I didn't get a good look."

Andrea was putting her scientific mind to work, so Jeremy knew it was useless. There was no doubt she had seen Flash, and even if he managed to distract her now, she was sure to tell Mom and Dad when they got home.

Jeremy slumped into a kitchen chair. "You're right," he said. "You saw Flash. I've known about him for a week and I've been feeding him and everything." He still had the raisins clenched in one fist.

"I knew I wasn't seeing things," Andrea said. "What kind is it? A field mouse, a house mouse?

I know it wasn't white like a laboratory mouse. It was dark. What do you feed it?" Andrea was excited now, almost as excited as Jeremy had been. Maybe it was OK for her to know.

Jeremy told her about the brownies and toast and bananas.

"Have you tried candy?" Andrea asked. "There was a mouse in Jamie's house and it got into her bag of Halloween candy. Her mom made her throw it all out.

"Boy," she continued, "I could get extra credit for a mouse dissection. Think we could catch it? It's kind of small but . . ."

"Cut it out, Andrea. No one is going to dissect Flash. He's my pet."

"Jeremy, you can't have a pet mouse that's just loose in the house. You don't even know where he lives. Besides, Mom doesn't allow pets. What is she going to say when she finds out?"

Jeremy stared hard at his sister. "She's not going to find out," he said very slowly and precisely. "Unless you tell her. Listen, Andrea, I got your weights for your science project. You owe me."

Andrea lowered her eyes. "I already stopped calling you Squirt, didn't I?"

"No, but you can call me Squirt. Just don't tell Mom about Flash."

"Flash," Andrea said. "That's a good name for

the rodent anyway. He sure is speedy." She hesitated. "All right, I won't say anything. But Mom's still going to find out, and she's not going to like it, especially when she hears you've been deliberately feeding him. You know how she is about leaving food around anyway." Andrea made a face. "Roaches and all."

"I'll think of something," Jeremy told her.

"Well, if we do have to trap him, make sure I get a good scientific observation before you dispose of him."

Jeremy cringed. "Don't tell anybody," he warned her as she headed back toward the phone. "Not even Jamie." Andrea was already in the closet.

Fat chance, Jeremy thought as he dumped the rest of the raisins into the trash.

Chapter 9

Andrea kept her promise and didn't say a thing about Flash when Mom and Dad got home. On Sunday at noon, she was setting the table for dinner, and Jeremy happened to walk into the kitchen just as she was opening the silverware drawer.

Jeremy saw her eyes get wide. He rushed over to her and slammed the drawer shut.

"Hey," Andrea started. "Did you see . . ." Jeremy put his finger to his lips and glanced over at Mom. She had her back to them. They were out of paper napkins so he grabbed a paper towel and waited for what he knew was coming.

"Jeremy, one piece at a time, and it better be necessary." Mom glanced around and turned back to the stove. It was like she had eyes in the back of her head.

"OK," Jeremy said, flashing Andrea a stare that meant *keep quiet*. Then he quickly opened the drawer and cleaned out the mouse droppings.

"Gross," Andrea mouthed at him as she continued to count out silver for the table, but she didn't say anything.

Flash must have sensed that everyone was home on Sunday because Jeremy didn't see his pet once all day. Jeremy was bored. He thought about drawing another invention, but he couldn't think of anything to invent, and he didn't feel like reading, so he wandered over to Mr. Applebaum's.

Mr. Applebaum was in the garage. "How's the mouse?" he asked.

"Fine," Jeremy told him. "At least as far as I know. Andrea saw him, but I don't think she's going to tell Mom."

"Uh-huh," Mr. Applebaum answered. "It's hard to keep a mouse a secret, I expect."

"Yeah," Jeremy agreed absently. He was looking at the giant empty spools piled up in one corner. They had been used for cables and wire. Jeremy thought the medium-size one would make a great table for his fort and the smaller one could be a chair. If he moved those out, maybe he could move some more of the stuff from the driveway back into the garage, where it wouldn't upset the neighbors so much.

Just as he was thinking about it, a kid came pushing his two-wheeler up the drive. The front tire was flat. Jeremy thought he was one of the Hull kids from down the street. He looked like he was about six or seven.

Jeremy watched as the boy wheeled his bike into the garage like he owned the place. He walked right past Jeremy, tossing him a "Hi," and went over to where Mr. Applebaum was working. "Can you fix my tire?" he asked the big man.

"What's the problem, son? Got yourself a flat? Sure, I guess I got some old tube here somewhere and some cee-ment." Jeremy didn't like to hear Mr. A. call someone else "son."

The boy watched as Mr. Applebaum removed the tire and pumped up the inner tube. Then he put it in some water and found the hole where the bubbles rose to the surface.

"Neat," said the boy.

It took only a few minutes and Mr. Applebaum had the tire pumped up and ready to roll. "There you go, son."

The boy hopped on his bike and propped himself up for a minute looking around the garage. He shook his head and said, "You sure have a lot of junk in here." Then he pushed off down the driveway.

Jeremy wondered if he should tell Mr. Applebaum that the kid's father wanted to file a complaint about the mess around his garage. Maybe he should tell his friend that fixing the kid's tire was a mistake. But he didn't. Instead, he asked if he could use the spools, and he spent the rest of the afternoon working on the fort.

On Monday morning Jeremy felt pretty good. His fort was coming along great. Mr. Applebaum was right when he said it was hard to keep a mouse a secret, but they'd made it through the weekend. Mom worked all week, so she wasn't so likely to see Flash during the day. That gave Jeremy some time to figure out what to do about his pet. He was whistling when he went downstairs for breakfast.

The pungent pine odor of disinfectant hit him at the bottom step, and he sensed something was wrong even before he reached the kitchen.

Mom was bent over the empty silverware drawer, scrubbing it with a sponge. One strand of hair fell down over her face and she looked upset.

Jeremy was afraid he knew what the problem was, but he hoped he was wrong. Maybe Mom had gotten up early to do some spring cleaning before work. "Hi, Mom. What's that smell?" he asked with a sinking feeling.

"Oh," Mom groaned. "You won't believe it, but we have a mouse. I opened the silverware drawer for a teaspoon and there were droppings all over."

She took another splash of disinfectant on her sponge and continued to scrub. "You'll have to grab something quick for breakfast. Wash the spoon and knife before you use them. The little beast has been climbing all over them. Who knows what diseases it carries. I don't have time for this."

Mom dried the drawer and placed several layers of paper towel in each section. She must have used nine pieces, so Jeremy knew this was serious.

He really wanted to tell Mom it was OK. They'd been eating off silver contaminated by a mouse for at least a week, probably a lot longer, and so far, everyone was alive and well. Instead, he said, "Mom, it's just a little mouse. It can't hurt anything. It's not like it's a rat or something."

"You're right," Mom said. "It could be a rat." She started washing the silverware. "But I think the droppings would be bigger. . . . I won't put anything back in the drawer until after I get a trap and catch the thing. I'll pick some up on the way home from work." Mom was talking to herself more than to Jeremy.

Jeremy suddenly lost his appetite for breakfast.

For all he knew, Flash would be crushed in a trap before he got home from school.

He could never tell Mom he'd been feeding Flash all week, but he had to tell her something. "Mom," he blurted out, "you can't trap him. He's my pet. His name is Flash."

"Jeremy!" Mom shrieked. "You knew about this mouse and didn't tell me?"

Just then Andrea came into the kitchen and sized up the situation immediately.

"So, Mom met Flash," she wisecracked. "It's OK, Mom. Jeremy takes all the responsibility for feeding him, and he even cleans up after him, and we don't have to worry about who's going to watch him when we go away."

"Andrea, you knew about this, too? Are there any more secrets you two would like to share?"

Jeremy made an angry face at his sister.

"Just trying to help," she told him as she helped herself to a banana. "Looks like the little varmint has been at the bananas. Neat, look at these little teeth marks in the half banana here."

"Oh, Andrea, throw it away. This is so embarrassing," Mom groaned.

Jeremy was getting desperate. "Listen, Mom, please don't set any traps."

"Jeremy, I can't let a mouse run free in this house. Those things make a mess. They chew everything up. Who knows what's been destroyed already? Not to mention the diseases they must carry. And what about fleas and ticks?"

"Mom, give me a few days. I'll think of something, I'll get rid of Flash, but you can't kill him. You haven't even seen him yet. He's cute with big ears and a pink tail."

"Listen," Andrea said collecting her books. "Jamie said they have sticky-paper traps for mice and you don't have to break their necks that way. But their fur gets all stuck and the mouse is still alive and struggles a long time before it dies and it's gross, too. Bye." Andrea was out the door.

"Mom," Jeremy said, desperately, "please promise me you won't set any traps before I get home."

"Well," Mom said, "if I stop to buy the traps, I won't get home until after you anyway. We'll discuss it then. But I warn you, I'm not living with a mouse in this house."

"Sure," Jeremy said. "I'll think of something." But he didn't really believe it.

Chapter 10

Jeremy had to run to catch the bus, so he didn't know if Robbie was there ahead of him. He perched on the edge of a front seat next to one of the little kids and tried to think of a way to save Flash.

Robbie was in math class though. "I heard your mom found out about the mouse," he told Jeremy. "She called my mom to say she'd be late to pick her up. I guess that's the end of your pet." Robbie slid into the seat across from Jeremy.

Jeremy couldn't tell whether Robbie was sympathizing, or trying to be mean. He didn't care. He was too busy trying to figure out what to do.

Jeremy wished he could talk to Mr. Applebaum. He'd have some ideas.

It was obvious, Flash couldn't live in their kitchen any longer. *Maybe Mom would let him stay in my bedroom,* Jeremy thought. How could he get Flash into his bedroom and make him stay? He would have to have a cage.

Mr. Cardillo was writing word problems on the board. Jeremy couldn't concentrate. Even if he got a cage, he'd still have to catch Flash. He needed something that wouldn't kill or torture a mouse but could still catch and hold him. Maybe a net. Or maybe he could just put the opening for the cage over the hole in the stove and wait for Flash to crawl in.

Jeremy couldn't believe it could be that simple. Why hadn't he thought of it before? After he went home to meet Mom, he was going directly to the pet shop to see about cages and maybe a net. He stopped doodling on his paper and tried to concentrate on his math.

Just then, there was a knock on the door. Mr. Stevens, the principal, came in. There was another man with him, but he stayed out in the hall. Mr. Stevens walked over to their teacher's desk and said something in a low voice. Mr. Cardillo raised his head and said, "Robbie, please go with Mr. Stevens."

Jeremy glanced at his friend. Robbie looked

confused and upset. Slowly he put his pencil down and stood up. He started to walk to the front of the classroom.

"You'll need your books," Mr. Stevens said. Robbie went back to his desk and scooped up all his papers and books. Jeremy could tell he was nervous. He didn't even straighten out his papers. As he stood up, Robbie glanced at Jeremy. Jeremy raised his hand in a little wave and Robbie followed the principal out of the room.

As soon as the door closed everyone started talking at once.

"What was that all about?" Michael asked.

"Looks like an execution," Jonathan said, laughing.

"Mr. Cardillo, tell us what's going on."

"This business is between Robbie and Mr. Stevens. Our business is to solve these math problems. Now settle down and get to work."

There was still another half hour of math class left. Mr. Stevens had made Robbie take his books, so he probably wasn't coming back for a while. It looked pretty serious, Jeremy thought. He had an uncomfortable feeling that it might have something to do with Robbie taking the candy at Mr. Dickson's. But that was last week, and how would Mr. Stevens know about it? Even though he was mad at Robbie, Jeremy felt sorry for him.

At lunchtime a few kids asked Jeremy if he

knew what was going on. There were a lot of rumors. Someone said the man with Mr. Stevens was a detective from the police department. Jeremy had never seen the man before, and he wouldn't have known if he was a detective. He didn't think the other kids knew either.

Someone else said Tom Morgan had been taken out of reading class and a couple of other sixth-graders, too. They said all of them got into a police car and they heard the sirens. Someone else said it was an unmarked car they left in. They even said the man had dark glasses and a gun. Jeremy didn't believe most of this, but he knew Robbie had been with Tom and one other kid on Saturday. Jeremy didn't tell anyone about that.

After lunch, everyone was restless. It seemed the whole school knew that Robbie and the other boys were in some sort of trouble. Jeremy couldn't keep his mind on work. Instead, he drew pictures of mouse cages, like the one he was going to buy this afternoon. He drew a picture of Flash, then drew a cage around him. Jeremy didn't like the way it looked, with bars, like a jail.

That made him think of Robbie again. What if Robbie was in trouble, real trouble, for stealing? What if Robbie went to jail? Jeremy knew they didn't put kids in jail, but what about juvenile detention or something? At the very least, he could be suspended from school or expelled.

Then Jeremy had a terrible thought. What if Robbie was in trouble for stealing the candy and he told the police Jeremy was there? Robbie probably wouldn't mean to tell, but maybe he would have to. Maybe they would torture him until he said Jeremy was an accomplice. Jeremy knew he should have told Mom right from the beginning.

The bell rang and Jeremy went to his bus. He waited to see if Robbie got on, but Robbie didn't show up. Neither did Tom nor his friend. *Maybe the kids were right,* Jeremy thought gloomily. *Maybe Robbie was arrested by a detective.* And maybe he was going to implicate Jeremy in the crime.

Chapter 11

Jeremy raced home from the bus stop wishing he had his bike. If he got home in time, he could clean up any mess Flash had left before Mom got home. Then maybe he'd still have a chance to talk Mom into letting him get a cage for his pet, instead of a trap.

Jeremy was concentrating so hard that he didn't notice Mom's car out in front of their house until he was practically on top of it. Even then he had to look twice to be sure it really was hers. What was she doing home so early? It was only ten past three and she never got home before twenty past. And why was the car outside? Mom always parked in the garage. What if she was in there setting traps for Flash? What if she had already caught him? Jeremy felt sick. He ran up the front steps and banged on the door. "Mom," he shouted. "Mom, Mom!"

"Jeremy," Mom exclaimed, opening the door.

Jeremy rushed past her into the kitchen. "You didn't set the traps, did you?" he called. "How come you got home so early?"

Mom followed him into the kitchen. "Jeremy, settle down," she said. "There's something I need to talk to you about." She took Jeremy by the shoulders and looked straight at him.

"Mom, you didn't get rid of Flash. You promised."

"No, Jeremy," she said calmly. "I forgot all about your mouse. Anne called me at work. There's a problem with Robbie. I left early so I could take her to the police station. And I was worried about you."

So Robbie must have said something. Jeremy sat down on the straight-backed wooden kitchen chair. "The principal came and took Robbie out of math class," he told his mother. "There was another man with him. Some kid said he was a detective." He hesitated. "But no one said anything to me."

"Well, from what Anne said, somebody took some red paint and made a real mess all over some of the shops in town, the pharmacy and a couple of others. Robbie says he wasn't involved, but they think he and two other boys did it. They found paint on those boys' clothes, and someone said they saw Robbie with them on the weekend. The other children's parents are not being co-operative with the police, and poor Anne is just a wreck. She doesn't know what to think. She knows Robbie was with them." Mom sounded upset.

Jeremy was speechless. It took him a minute to change gears. So this wasn't about the candy. Robbie was in some other kind of trouble. "When did it happen?" he asked.

"Sometime on Sunday evening. Anne says she was out on a date with Russ and she doesn't actually know where Robbie was. He says he was at home."

"Where did they get the paint?"

"That's the other thing I need to talk to you about. When I got home there was a patrol car at the Applebaums' house and a few of the neighbors were standing around. It seems those boys got the paint from his garage. They made quite a mess over there, too. Although it's hard to tell," she added.

"Oh, no." Jeremy jumped up. "What did they do? Is Mr. Applebaum OK?"

"I'm sure he's fine, but he's got some work to do. There's some paint spilled."

Jeremy was angry now. Robbie and those kids had been snooping around on Saturday. First shoplifting and now this.

"Jeremy," Mom continued, "you don't know anything about this, do you? You don't know where Robbie was on Sunday?"

"No," Jeremy said. "I was at Mr. Applebaum's." He didn't know anything about Robbie lately, and it was too late to tell Mom about the shoplifting. That's not what this was about anyway.

"I know you two boys haven't been getting along lately, and now this," Mom said. "I just can't understand what's gotten into Robbie. I feel bad for Anne. She doesn't know what to do."

"Mom," Jeremy said, "I've got to get over to Mr. Applebaum's. He might need my help." Jeremy wanted to see for himself what those kids had done.

"I know you're concerned about Mr. Applebaum, but maybe you shouldn't bother him right now."

"I don't bother him," Jeremy protested. "Mr. Applebaum is my friend. I have to go make sure everything is OK."

Mom gave Jeremy a hug. "It must have been upsetting for you when they took Robbie out of class. I suppose it's all right to go next door and take a look, but don't stay too long."

This was no time for diving through the

hedges. Jeremy went around and up the driveway. Mr. A. was on his knees with a scrub brush in the middle of a huge red stain right in front of the garage. A heap of soggy scarlet rags nearby was evidence that there had been more than a few splashes to clean up.

Mr. Applebaum looked up at Jeremy. "We had some mischief here last night," he said. "Blame kids made a mess. I'd like to get my hands on those boys."

Jeremy lowered his eyes. He didn't want Mr. Applebaum to know he knew one of those kids. "Can I help?" he asked.

"I'm pretty much done here." Jeremy looked around. The paint cans were scattered all over in front of the garage and the pipes were spattered with red paint. Jeremy was embarrassed to remember he hadn't cleaned them up on Saturday. He picked up two long ones and started to make a neat pile.

"Hey you, boy. What kind of trouble you going to get into now? Samuel, why do you let him here after the mess he made?" Mrs. Applebaum was on the back porch. She was shaking her finger at Jeremy.

"Oh, leave the boy alone," Mr. Applebaum told her. "He didn't do nothing."

"He's a troublemaker and that's the truth. His momma should keep him home." She slammed the screen door and was gone. Jeremy half expected her to pop out again any second.

"That woman's been after me all day to get this mess cleaned up." Mr. Applebaum shook his head. "I expect she's got plenty more to say, too." He winked at Jeremy. "Nope, I sure enough haven't heard the end of this. But you don't need to pay her no mind."

Jeremy smiled halfheartedly at his friend, then picked up several more pipes and took them around to the side door of the garage. When he glanced at his fort, he noticed that the two doors were crooked and the toilet seat was missing. He put the pipes down and went over to investigate. The pink toilet seat was a few feet away in the garden, nearly on top of Mr. Applebaum's little greenhouse.

Those kids, Jeremy thought, *have been inside my fort. They've practically destroyed it, and it's all Robbie's fault.* He gripped the toilet seat hard. He felt like throwing it at somebody. He wanted to scream at Robbie and tell him what a jerk he was.

Jeremy tossed the toilet seat back down on the doors. The whole fort shook, and some of the dirt caved in on one side. It was hardly worth fixing up. He could tell without looking inside. His fort was ruined. He didn't want to think about it. Jeremy picked up the pipes and looked around the garage for a place to pile them, but there wasn't any room. He put them back outside with the other pipes and rearranged the pile by size as well as he could.

At dinner, Jeremy listened while Mom told Dad and Andrea about Robbie and the paint. Andrea said she didn't know how, but some of the kids in middle school already knew about it and there had been rumors all day. "My teacher saw the graffiti on Mr. Dickson's store," she said, "and she thinks whoever did it should be made to pay for it."

"I have to agree with her," Dad said. "I'm only sorry that Robbie had to be involved. I never thought of him as someone who would destroy other people's property."

"They say it will take several thousand dollars to clean it up," Mom added. "Anne says Robbie's been acting strange ever since he came back from his dad's."

Jeremy wondered if she knew just how strange.

"So, what happened about the mouse?" Andrea asked.

Flash! Jeremy hadn't thought about his pet since he'd gotten home.

"Oh, dear," Mom said. "I forgot all about getting the traps. I'll have to do it tomorrow."

"Mom," Jeremy told her, "I've got it all figured out. We can get a cage and put it over the burner. That's where he gets in and out. And then we can catch him, and I can keep him in my room. I can take care of him and it won't be any problem, I promise."

"Hold on," Dad said. "What's this about a mouse?"

Mom told him she had seen mouse droppings and had cleaned the drawer and all the silverware before work.

"And Jeremy has been feeding him for a week or more," Andrea added.

"Jeremy," Dad said, "catching a mouse by putting a cage over his hole won't work. It's just not practical. You'd have to leave it there and wait for the mouse, and he wouldn't come out if you were watching for him."

Jeremy knew Dad was right, but he just couldn't let them kill his pet. "Dad," Jeremy said plaintively, "his name is Flash. He has big ears and a pink tail and he eats peanut butter and bananas."

"Well," Dad said, "I have a suggestion. They have traps that catch the mouse alive. The animal goes in for the food and tips the trap so the door closes. If we caught him, we could take him up to the baseball field or down to the cemetery and let him go. What do you say?"

Jeremy thought for a minute. Letting Flash go meant he wouldn't have a pet of his own anymore, but at least they wouldn't have to hurt him.

"OK," he told Dad.

"That's settled, then," Mom said. "I'll buy the traps tomorrow. I'm sure I can get them at the hardware store. But I refuse to be the one to have to empty the trap once we catch the creature."

"I'll do it," Andrea volunteered.

"No way," Jeremy told her. "Flash is my pet. I'll be the one to let him go." Jeremy was beginning to feel better than he had felt all day.

Chapter 12

Robbie wasn't at the bus stop the next day and he wasn't in school. Jeremy thought it was probably a good thing. Everybody was talking about how Robbie and his friends had been accused of vandalizing the pharmacy and some other shops. Some kids said that the hardware store had been broken into and the suspects had used spray paint they found there to do their damage.

Jeremy knew they hadn't used spray paint and it hadn't come from the hardware store, but he didn't tell anyone. He was still furious at Robbie. Robbie didn't have any business bringing those kids over to the garage. He should have never stolen the paint. He almost wished Robbie had been in school so he could let him have it about making trouble for Mr. Applebaum.

Jeremy didn't join the discussion. He felt uncomfortable adding to the gossip, even though he figured he probably had the most reliable information.

There had been a short article about the incident in the morning paper. It said there were three suspects, but it hadn't mentioned any names, although the article did say it was believed they had gotten the paint from the home of a Mr. S. Applebaum on Hilldale Drive. It gave the boys' ages and said the case was being handled by the juvenile authorities. Of course everyone knew who the boys were, but no one seemed to know that Jeremy lived next door to Mr. Applebaum. It was just as well, Jeremy thought. He wanted to keep his friend out of this as much as possible.

Andrew Webber said he heard Robbie and Tom and another boy were going to be expelled from school and that they would have to go to reform school. Randy Smith's father worked at the police station, and Randy said the boys had been suspended from school until they went to court. Could they really take a kid to court like that? Who would be Robbie's lawyer? Jeremy wondered if Mr. Applebaum would have to go to court to testify or something. That would be awful. Jeremy didn't want Mr. Applebaum to have any more trouble. What if detectives had to come to his house for questioning and evidence? What if Mr. Applebaum got into trouble because it was his paint?

Jeremy had a hard time concentrating on his schoolwork. He was worried about Flash, too. He had forgotten to tell Mom to wait until he got home before she set the new traps. But Jeremy figured he could get home before her, easily, unless she left work early again.

At least Mom's car was not in front of the house when Jeremy came up the street. He let himself in the back door quietly, hoping Flash might be out and he could catch a glimpse of him. Jeremy wanted to see his mouse one more time before he had to trap him and let him go.

Flash wasn't there. Jeremy tried to remember the last time he had seen his pet. He hoped nothing had happened to him inside the stove.

"I've got the traps," Mom said when she got home. "I bought two so we can set them in two different areas of the kitchen. Maybe one should go in the silverware drawer, although I don't know if it will fit."

Jeremy took one of the traps out of its packaging. It was an oblong brown plastic container a little bigger than a mouse. He read the directions and examined the trap more closely. It was simple. You put the bait back inside the box and then set the prop so the container tilted forward. When the mouse went for the food, the container would tilt back and the door could swing down and shut so it couldn't get out.

What a clever invention, Jeremy thought. If only he could think of something that simple and useful to design.

"I saw the mess at the hardware store," Mom said as he unwrapped the second trap. "It's going to take some cleaning up and a new paint job. I can't help thinking that if Mr. Applebaum hadn't had all that paint outside his garage, those boys wouldn't have been able to get into so much trouble."

"Mom," Jeremy protested, "you can't say this is Mr. Applebaum's fault. They had no business stealing his paint."

"Of course. I know you're right, Jeremy. I just feel so bad for Anne. Robbie still says he didn't do it and she really doesn't know what to believe.

"And then there were those . . ." Mom hesitated for a minute. "Anne found some, ah— pictures, and ah, magazines under Robbie's bed."

Jeremy was embarrassed. "I know, Mom. He showed me one." They were both silent for a minute. He knew she was upset so he added, "I wasn't interested."

Mom came over and gave Jeremy a hug. She held him hard for a minute and Jeremy put the trap down. "I know this has been difficult for you," she said. "I guess Robbie hasn't been much of a friend these last couple of weeks, and I didn't understand. I'm glad you knew enough to stay away from trouble. Maybe when this blows over, you'll be able to help Robbie. I think he's going to need a friend, someone he can depend on."

Jeremy murmured some agreement and busied himself with the mousetraps. How did Mom think he was going to be friends with Robbie again? Robbie obviously didn't want to be friends with him, and Jeremy was too mad to be friends anyway. He didn't want Robbie to go to reform school or anything. He just wanted him to stay away.

Chapter 13

Jeremy changed and got himself a snack. He knew he was really avoiding what he had to do. He set one of the traps down on the counter and tilted the opening down with the prop. Then he tipped the trap back. Clank. The door slid down over the opening.

"They told me at the hardware store to use peanut butter or fruit," Mom said.

"Flash likes peanut butter and bananas," Jeremy told her. He hated the idea of tricking his pet with his favorite food, but he didn't have any choice. In the end Jeremy supposed it would be for his own good. He took two small round slices of banana and spread some peanut butter on each. Carefully, he slid one slice into the back of each trap. He propped one trap up on the counter, right on the edge by the stove. The other one he put near the fruit bowl.

"Let's hope that does the trick," Mom said.

"He probably won't come out until tonight," Jeremy told her.

"You're right," Mom said, "but I'd like to get this taken care of as soon as possible."

Jeremy wanted to get it over with, too, but it was no use sitting around waiting for Flash to appear. "I'll be over at Mr. Applebaum's. Let me know as soon as we catch him," he told Mom. Jeremy hated the idea of Flash being in that tiny trap for too long. It obviously wasn't airtight, but it would be terribly frightening for the mouse, he was sure.

Jeremy saw the patrol car in Applebaum's driveway as soon as he walked around the corner of the house. It was parked with the driver's door open at the end of the driveway. The back end of the car stuck out into the street. That was as far as you could get a car into the driveway.

Not more trouble, he thought. Maybe they really were going to make Mr. Applebaum go to court. Or maybe they just needed the paint for evidence.

Jeremy squeezed between the car and the

hedge and walked down the driveway. He could see two police officers with Mr. and Mrs. Applebaum. Then he saw Mr. Hull with them and Mrs. Sullivan standing at the back gate with her grass clippers in one hand. Mr. Hull was talking.

Jeremy walked slowly up to the group. One of the officers turned to look at him, then turned back to the others without saying a word. They were looking at Jeremy's fort.

"I want this whole place cleaned up," Mr. Hull said, angrily. "I knew something should have been done about it sooner. I'm not going to sue him. I just want to make the neighborhood safe for my kids. I guess I'd have a case, though. Look at this pit. Boards all over. Anyone can see it was an accident waiting to happen."

Jeremy wanted to know what Mr. Hull was talking about, but he couldn't ask. No one paid any attention to him. Mr. Applebaum just hung his head down. Jeremy wondered what Mr. Hull was so angry about. What did he mean about su-ing, anyway?

"It's lucky my son was here to come and get me or my little girl would still be in there." Mr. Hull nodded toward the fort again, and Jeremy noticed that all the boards had been taken off and laid to one side. "She never could have got-ten out by herself," Mr. Hull continued. "She's got a fractured arm and she's lucky it wasn't worse. Now I want the hole filled in, and I want this place cleaned up, or I'll be speaking to my lawyer."

"My land." Mrs. Applebaum spoke up in a shaky voice. "I been telling him we were going to have trouble with this mess." She clutched her apron skirt and then threw her hands up in despair. "It'll sure enough get cleaned up, now," she added in a stronger voice. She looked at her husband.

Mr. Applebaum nodded. "We'll get it cleaned up," he said quietly.

"I don't think there will be any trouble here," one of the officers said to Mr. Hull. "You can get home to your little girl now."

"Thank you, officer," Mr. Hull said.

It had begun to dawn on Jeremy what had happened. This wasn't about the paint in town at all. It had to do with his fort, and somebody falling in and breaking an arm, and Mr. Applebaum almost getting sued.

He watched as Mr. Applebaum offered his big rough hand to shake with Mr. Hull. "I'm sure sorry about your little girl," he said.

But it's not your fault, Jeremy wanted to shout. *I did it. I made the hole. Mr. Applebaum even said we should fill it in and I begged him to leave it.*

Mr. Hull shook hands, nodded, and walked down the driveway. The older officer, the man with the gray hair, turned to Mr. Applebaum. "Well, Samuel, you better get that hole filled in, and then this place is going to have to be cleaned up. He's got a point. He could probably take you to court, and this isn't the first time we've had complaints. With those boys getting that paint here and now this, I'm afraid I'll have to give you a warning."

"I guess you're right, Gus," Mr. Applebaum said slowly.

"We'll have this mess hauled away, officer, quick as you like," Mrs. Applebaum interrupted.

"I can arrange for a dumpster, if you want," said the officer.

"Thanks, Gus," Mr. Applebaum replied. The police officer headed down the driveway.

"Looks like we're going to get this place cleaned up," Mrs. Applebaum called across to Mrs. Sullivan on the other side of the gate.

" 'Bout time," Mrs. Sullivan said, and turned back to her clipping.

"What're you gawking at?" Mrs. Applebaum asked as she noticed Jeremy. "You git on home." She headed toward the back steps.

"Leave the boy alone," Mr. Applebaum told his wife. "He don't do no harm."

They were alone. Mr. Applebaum didn't speak to Jeremy. He just stood looking around at his garden. Jeremy thought maybe he should go, but he didn't want to leave. "I'll fill in the hole," he said finally.

"No need," Mr. Applebaum said. "I got lots of time and two good hands."

Jeremy hesitated. "But . . . but it was my fault."

"Aw, don't talk that way," Mr. Applebaum told him. "It's nobody's fault. It was an accident, is all." He pulled the shovel out of the dirt where it had been left standing in the garden and started filling in the fort with the dark soil.

Jeremy stood listening to the steady rhythm of Mr. Applebaum's work. Scoop and heave. Scrape and thud. He saw that the job would be done quickly, but he needed to help. He ran to the garage and came back with another shovel.

It made him feel better working alongside Mr. Applebaum. Silently he fell into his own rhythm. He couldn't help thinking, if only he had done this a few days earlier, none of this would have happened.

When they finished, Jeremy scraped his shovel across the soil to make it even. "Are you really going to get rid of everything?" he asked Mr. Applebaum.

Mr. Applebaum looked back toward the garage and driveway. "Reckon I got to," he said. "Most of it, leastways. Not much good to no one anyway." Then he winked at Jeremy. "Won't hurt to make this place a mite prettier."

Jeremy wished he could wink back. When he tried, he always squinted up both eyes and the whole side of his face. Instead, he smiled a crooked half smile at his friend. He was glad Mr. Applebaum didn't blame him, but he still felt responsible.

Jeremy walked home slowly, wondering if they were really going to get rid of everything in the garage or just neaten things up, maybe get rid of some of the stuff outside. How would they ever clear all that stuff out? It was going to take years.

Jeremy couldn't understand how that little kid could have fallen into his fort. Andrea had jumped on the fort, for crying out loud, and she didn't fall in. Jeremy knew he had made it sturdy. Then he remembered something. On Monday, after Robbie and those guys had gotten into the paint, he had noticed the fort had been messed with. That's right, the toilet seat had been thrown off and everything. That's why that little girl had fallen in. They had moved the doors. Should he tell someone whose fault this all really was? Now that he knew what had happened, maybe Mr. Applebaum wouldn't have to clean everything up. Jeremy wondered if Robbie knew just how much trouble he had caused.

If Robbie were here now, he thought, he'd tell him off good. Who cared what kind of problems Robbie had now? He deserved all of them. Jeremy wanted to strangle him.

<u>Chapter</u> 14

Jeremy was up early the next morning. He wanted to check the traps and have time to release Flash before school. The traps had remained untouched the day before, but Jeremy hadn't expected Flash to come out and investigate something new like that while people were still up in the house. He had put fresh peanut butter and banana in each trap, and he was sure Flash would be there this morning. He didn't want his mouse to spend more time in that little trap than he had to, even if it meant letting him go.

The trap by the fruit bowl was still propped up

and open, but the one next to the burner was tipped forward and closed. Jeremy knew Flash was there.

For a second he was almost disappointed. He had spent so much time trying to get a good look at his pet, and now that he'd finally found a simple way to catch him, he had to let him go. He thought again about keeping Flash in a cage, but he knew Mom would never let him. Even Dad wasn't on his side, and there was no way he wanted to let Andrea get ahold of Flash. So Jeremy took a deep breath and walked quickly but quietly over to the trap.

He wondered if Flash was sleeping. He was probably scared to death. Jeremy didn't want to startle him, so he picked the trap up very carefully and gently.

Right away Jeremy could tell the little box felt too light for Flash to be in there, but he had to be sure. Slowly he raised the door, half expecting to see a tail poking out. But no, the trap was empty. Even the banana and peanut butter were gone. But Flash was not there. First Jeremy thought maybe he hadn't opened the door when he set the trap or maybe Mom or Dad or someone had bumped it closed, but that didn't explain why the banana was gone.

Flash must have gotten the banana without getting caught, Jeremy realized, feeling proud of his clever mouse. Jeremy also knew that if Flash was smart enough to keep from getting caught by these traps, his cleverness was going to get the mouse into trouble. Sooner or later, Jeremy consoled himself, the catch-'em-alive traps would work. This had only been the first night.

"Someone's been up before me," Dad said as he came into the kitchen. "Any luck?" he added when he saw Jeremy with the trap.

"Yes and no," Jeremy said. He explained about how the one trap had been tipped, but Flash got away.

Dad examined the trap and Jeremy showed him where he had put it.

"Where are the directions?" Dad asked.

"I don't have them. I think we threw them out," Jeremy told him.

"Well, I think the trap is supposed to work best if it is up against the wall or baseboard," Dad said. "Next time, try putting it here." Dad pushed the trap back on the counter, against the wall. "I know you wanted it next to the opening, but if that mouse wants the bait, he'll find it here."

"Thanks," Jeremy said. He reset both traps with banana and tried to put them against the wall.

When Mom came down, she was sorry to hear that Flash was still loose. There were more droppings in the silverware drawer and on the counter. She had already moved the fruit bowl into the dining room so Flash couldn't get the bananas.

Dad reassured Mom and Jeremy as he left for work. "I expect it will take a couple of tries, but I don't think the culprit will remain at large for long." Mom made a face and Jeremy laughed.

But Jeremy wasn't laughing when he walked down the driveway on his way to school. Right there, smack in front of Mr. Applebaum's house, was a huge green dumpster. It was almost as long as the width of the front yard. Two men Jeremy had never seen before were hauling the pipes and paint cans down the driveway.

Jeremy stood still and watched as the men started carrying the sections of conveyer rollers down to the dumpster. Jeremy wanted to yell, "Wait! I was going to make a roller coaster with those."

He wondered where Mr. Applebaum was. He was about to take a quick look for him when Mom stuck her head out the front door.

"Jeremy, it's eight-fifteen. You'll miss the bus."

"OK, Mom," Jeremy said. Instead of going to Mr. Applebaum's, he headed down the sidewalk in the opposite direction. He almost wished he would miss the bus. Then he could go back to Applebaum's. Maybe his friend would need him for something. But what could Jeremy do? Besides, if he skipped school, he could get into trouble.

He glanced back one more time and saw the man rolling two large tractor-trailer tires down the driveway. No, Jeremy knew he couldn't go back. He couldn't risk getting Mr. A. into more trouble. He already had enough of that because of Jeremy.

Jeremy felt sick. At first he had thought no one could ever get rid of all the stuff in Mr. Applebaum's garage. After seeing the huge dumpster and those two men moving so fast, he wasn't sure. What if they had it all done before he got home from school? He wouldn't have a chance to see if there were some things he needed. What about all those buttons and spools and wires he had thought he might be able to use? Immediately, he felt guilty for thinking about himself and wondered about the chickens. Would they really get rid of the chickens, too?

Robbie wasn't in school, but Jeremy hadn't expected to see him. Mom had said that Mrs. Fuller told her she was keeping Robbie out of school until they had been to court and things blew over a bit. It seemed like everyone at school had already forgotten about the whole incident, but Jeremy couldn't forget for a minute. The more he thought about how Mr. Hull had talked to Mr. Applebaum and the way Mr. Applebaum just hung his head, the worse Jeremy felt. Jeremy was almost as mad at himself as he was at Robbie. He should have filled the fort in when Mr. Applebaum suggested it. But how could he know Robbie would bring those kids back? Who did Robbie think he was, anyway? Stealing and destroying property and lying! Jeremy couldn't believe Robbie had ever been his friend. It all went around in his head until Jeremy closed his eyes and wished it would all go away. He wished things could go back to the way they were before spring vacation.

In math class, Mr. Cardillo gave them an interesting problem to solve. It was about a man in an elevator, not really a math problem, but Mr. Cardillo said it was good brain exercise. Jeremy liked that kind of problem, and he was glad to have something else to think about for a change.

After school, Jeremy was anxious to get over to Mr. Applebaum's. On the way home, he was still trying to figure out why the man in the problem got off the elevator at the fifth floor. When he entered the kitchen and was facing the two traps, he realized he had totally forgotten about Flash. The doors of both traps were snapped shut. But as soon as he picked them up, Jeremy could tell that they were both empty. Once again, Flash had enjoyed the bait and avoided getting trapped.

One smart mouse, Jeremy thought grimly. *Too*

smart for his own good. Still, he couldn't help smiling when he saw a bit of banana and peanut butter Flash had pulled over to the burner. *Sorry, Flash,* he thought, *I've got to clean this up before Mom gets home.*

The dumpster was still out in front of Applebaum's, but now there were two old pickup trucks and a beat-up station wagon parked across the street. Jeremy squeezed through the hedges to avoid the two men in the driveway sorting pipes. He walked across the yard and peeked in the side door of the garage.

Mrs. Applebaum was standing inside with her back to him, a little bowlegged in black shoes with thick pump heels. Her elbows stuck out to the sides as she rested her fists on her hips. In the light that came through the doorway, Jeremy noticed she had a bald spot in the back of her fine gray hair. She was giving orders to the men. "Leave some of them tools, one of each least-ways, so as we can still do repairs. I'll get to straightening them up."

One of the men was kind of young and he wore painter's pants. He held six or seven doorknobs in the crook of one arm, and with his other hand he was raking through a big pile of others. A cigarette hung out of the corner of his mouth. Jeremy could see a tattoo on his upper arm, but he couldn't make the design out.

"Did you check those buttons, Jim?" he called to one of the other men. Jeremy didn't hear his reply.

He was shocked at how empty the garage looked. Even from the partial view he had, he could tell almost everything was gone. The yard and drive looked bare and hardly recognizable.

Jeremy walked around the back to the garden, where he found Mr. Applebaum squatting down bent over some seedlings. He looked old and tired. Suddenly, Jeremy didn't know what to say to his friend.

Before he could speak, Mr. Abbottello came to the side fence. "Samuel," he called. "I see you're gettin' the place cleaned up. That's a fine idea."

Mr. Applebaum stood and nodded his head absently, in agreement. He caught sight of Jeremy, and he reached toward him in a beckoning gesture. Jeremy took several steps toward him and Mr. Applebaum rested an arm over his shoulders. "Hey, son," he said quietly.

"Listen, Samuel," Mr. Abbottello went on. "I was wondering if I could take a look at your hubcaps. Just noticed this morning I'm missing one. Don't know when I lost the blame thing. Thought maybe you had a match."

"The hubcaps are gone," Jeremy said crossly before Mr. Applebaum could speak.

"Well, now," Mr. Abbottello said, shaking his

116

head. "That's too bad. Thought I might be a little late." He stood for a moment with his hand on the fence, gazing thoughtfully at the garage, and then turned back toward his own house.

Mr. Applebaum turned back to his work in the garden and began humming his song. Today it sounded more melancholy than ever.

Jeremy stooped to pull a few small weeds, the way Mr. Applebaum was doing, but he knew the few blades of grass were too tiny to worry about. He stood up again, resting his hands on his hips. Then, feeling very aware that he had nothing to do with his hands, he dropped them to his sides.

He looked around. There was no extra hoe or rake in the garden, and the hose was curled neatly in a pile by the spigot. There was nothing to do out here, and there were too many strangers in the garage.

Jeremy wanted to tell Mr. Applebaum about Flash, and the trap that caught mice alive, and how Flash was too smart to get caught. Somehow, it was too quiet, and he knew his voice would sound too loud if he spoke. Jeremy was used to being quiet with Mr. Applebaum. He had never felt uncomfortable before. He stood awkwardly for a few more moments and then turned to go.

"See ya," he called over his shoulder, but he didn't think Mr. Applebaum heard him.

"Hey," Andrea called as Jeremy squeezed back

through the hedges. "I was just coming to look for you. Do you think Mr. Applebaum has any wood for a puppet stage over there? We're writing a puppet show for English, and I told Mrs. Buckingham I could get some wood for the stage. We're making the puppets in art class and if it turns out good enough, we get to come back to Manor Day to put it on for you guys."

"There's nothing left over there," Jeremy told her as he walked past her toward the house.

"Come on, Jer. There must be a few pieces of wood."

Couldn't she see for herself? The dumpster was practically full. "It's all gone," Jeremy told her. "Now get off my case." The back door slammed behind him.

Chapter 15

The dumpster sat out in the street in front of Mr. Applebaum's for the rest of the week. It was full to overflowing. The pickup truck and station wagon didn't come back after the second day, but on Thursday, a green truck from a landscaping company pulled up next door. Two men got out with lawn mowers and hedge clippers and started to work in Mr. Applebaum's yard.

Jeremy watched for a minute from his own yard. Mr. Applebaum was nowhere in sight. Jeremy wondered what his friend was doing, but he didn't go over. There was nothing for him to do over there by himself, and he couldn't imagine going up to the door to ask. He didn't want to talk to Mrs. Applebaum, and if Mr. Applebaum came to the door himself, Jeremy wouldn't know what to say.

The next week, Robbie still wasn't in school. He was having schoolwork sent home to him, and Mom heard from Mrs. Fuller that he was due in court on Friday. Mom told Jeremy that Robbie still said he wasn't with the other boys, but there was no proof. The other boys told the police he showed them where to get the paint. That just confirmed what Jeremy already suspected, and fueled his anger. When Mom suggested he might want to go visit Robbie, he didn't even answer her.

On Thursday evening, Jeremy was doing his homework in the kitchen. He knew Flash was still around, because Mom was seeing more and more droppings and getting more and more upset. Those catch-'em-alive traps just didn't seem to work for Flash. Jeremy had tried different bait, including cheese and brownies, but nothing seemed to work.

When he finished his homework, Jeremy went downstairs to look for some scraps of wood and tools. Their basement was nothing like Mr. Applebaum's garage, but he was hoping he could get an idea for something to invent, something to take his mind off Flash and Mr. Applebaum. Dad was busy at his workbench.

"I'm trying to fix this old lamp for your

mother," Dad told him. "I don't know if it's worth it. She says it's an antique, but to tell you the truth, I can't always tell an antique from junk."

"Yeah." Jeremy smiled. He recognized the lamp as one of Mom's favorites.

"Now," Dad said. "I think if I had some electrical tape, that would do it. Any chance Mr. Applebaum has some left over there in his garage?"

Jeremy shook his head. "Dad," he said desolately, "there's nothing over there. It's all gone. I haven't even seen Mr. Applebaum."

"Nick and Jeremy, will you come up here and look at this?" Mom was calling from the head of the stairs. "It's this mouse. I'm not going to put up with this any longer."

Dad raised his eyebrows at Jeremy. "Sounds like we're wanted immediately."

Mom met them at the top of the stairs. She was holding a red-and-blue-flowered dish towel with several ragged holes in it. "I just opened my linen drawer here to get a clean towel, and look at this. That's not the only one." She held up a blue terry dish cloth and another towel. Both were in shreds.

"And," she continued, pulling open the next drawer which held paper goods, "look at this."

Jeremy and his father peered into the open bottom drawer. There were bits of paper napkins, paper towel, and tinfoil all chewed and balled up together.

"Looks like your mouse has been building himself a nest," Dad said.

"I'd say he's been quite busy," Mom added grimly. "Something has got to be done."

"What's all the commotion?" Andrea asked as she appeared out of the hall closet.

"Jeremy's mouse has gotten himself into a little trouble with your mom." Dad pointed to the mess.

"That's nothing," Andrea told them. "Jamie was just telling me that when they had a mouse last summer, her mom had been serving iced tea to some guests and they had already been drinking it, even. When it got near the bottom, she went to stir it, and guess what she found? A dead mouse. Can you imagine? Gross."

"Well, that's one way to catch a mouse, but drowning means he's definitely dead," Dad said.

Jeremy just scowled at Andrea.

"This is not a joke," Mom said. "We are going to have to try something else."

"There's always the sticky trap, like Jamie used," Andrea said helpfully. "It's kind of like fly paper, I think. When the mouse goes for the food he gets stuck. He doesn't die right away, but I don't know how you'd get him off the trap alive. He still would make a good specimen though."

"Shut up, Andrea!" Jeremy yelled.

"Andrea, Jeremy," Mom said sternly. "That's enough."

"Mom," Jeremy said, "we can't use a sticky trap on Flash, and he isn't a specimen."

"Listen," Dad said, "I'm sure those traps will work eventually. Sooner or later, Flash is bound to make a mistake. Why don't we give it until the first of next week? It's only a few more days, and maybe by then we'll think of something."

"Thanks, Dad," Jeremy told his father as he followed him back down the stairs.

"I've just bought you a little time," Dad said. "I'm not at all sure those traps are going to work in the next few days. Let's face it, Jeremy, either your mouse is too clever, or there's a bug in the design of those traps. I'll check at the hardware store and see what they suggest. You might want to ask at the pet store and see if they have any ideas."

"Sure," Jeremy said, but he wasn't very hopeful.

Jeremy hadn't been to town since the day Robbie and his friends had been accused of vandalism. When he bicycled in on Friday, after school, he noticed faint red splotches still visible on the sidewalk in front of the drugstore and hardware store. He couldn't make out the words. The outside of the buildings had been washed down, but they still showed traces of red paint. A man with a bucket and long window squeegee was scraping and washing the drugstore windows. Jeremy thought about going in to buy a candy bar, but he still felt uncomfortable having to face Mr. Dickson. Besides, he wanted to save his money in case he had to buy something at the pet store, so he kept going. Jeremy could see that some red paint had been splashed on the pet-store door. Mom had said that most of the shop owners were waiting to see what the judge decided in court today before they repainted.

Robbie was probably on the judge's stand right now. Maybe the boys had already been sentenced. Jeremy wondered if they had been handcuffed, and if people tried to take their pictures when they went into the courthouse. That would be awful. Jeremy hoped that hadn't happened to Robbie, even if he was a jerk.

Inside the pet shop, Jeremy stopped by the mouse cages. None of the mice looked like Flash. A lot of them were white. Jeremy didn't like the white ones. They reminded him of laboratory mice, and he knew people did awful things to laboratory mice. There were gray mice, too, lighter gray than Flash. Jeremy thought Flash was handsomer and cuter. There were some tiny mice that must have been younger than the others. They were cute, too.

"We don't have too much experience catching wild mice," the man behind the counter told Jeremy when he described the problem. "You might try using raisins or peanuts. Sometimes the little critters like that."

It wasn't much to work on, Jeremy thought as he rode his bike home. He'd have to give the peanuts a try, though. He'd have to try anything at this point if he was going to save Flash by the beginning of next week.

Jeremy walked his bike up the driveway and looked over the hedge into Mr. Applebaum's yard. It looked like a different place. The hedges were trimmed and the grass was cut. The rose bush against the side of the garage was cut back and neat-looking instead of bushing out all over. Jeremy liked it better the old way. The garage even had a new coat of white paint.

Jeremy stretched up on tiptoes, but he couldn't see Mr. Applebaum anywhere in his yard. He hadn't seen him for more than a week. What he could see was that Mr. Applebaum's vegetable garden was beginning to get a few weeds. *Mr. A. would never let a weed grow in his garden*, Jeremy thought, and suddenly he was worried about his friend. He missed him. Where could he be? Maybe he was still in the garage, or around the corner in the garden.

Jeremy squeezed through the neatly trimmed hedges and walked across to the garage. The side door was locked. Jeremy had never seen it closed before.

He went around to the front, where the door was rolled up, and edged past Mr. Applebaum's station wagon, which was parked inside the garage. Jeremy could hardly recognize the place. Except for the car, it was almost completely empty. On the walls were some new shiny hooks with a rake and shovel and clippers hanging on them, and a green hose wrapped neatly in a circle. The floor had been swept perfectly clean and was a nearly white cement color like any sidewalk.

Jeremy felt awful. Mr. Applebaum's garage looked just like anybody else's garage. It was even neater than Jeremy's family's garage. Everything was gone. Everything.

Jeremy had to get outside again. He had to get some air. Even though he knew Mr. Applebaum wouldn't be there, he walked to the part of the garden behind the garage. The little plants inside Mr. A.'s greenhouse were starting to wilt. *They haven't been watered all week,* Jeremy thought. He lifted the piece of glass and carefully set it aside. He looked around, and then remembered the hose was in the garage. He cupped his hands at the spigot and carried some water to the hole where the green seedlings were growing. He made several more trips with the water dripping through his fingers, and then covered the hole again with the glass.

"Howdy," a voice called behind him. Jeremy turned. It was Mr. Abbottello from across the fence. "Is Samuel over there?"

Jeremy shook his head.

"I thought he might be able to help me get my air conditioner working before it gets too hot."

"I haven't seen him for a few days," Jeremy told him.

Mr. Abbottello shook his head. "I was sure he'd be able to give me a hand. It maybe just needs a new switch."

Jeremy didn't say anything, and Mr. Abbottello walked back toward his house. Then he stopped and turned back toward Jeremy. "He's OK, isn't he? Samuel isn't sick or anything?"

"I don't know." Jeremy felt helpless.

Mr. Abbottello pulled at his chin. "It's not like Samuel to leave his garden go."

Jeremy sighed and walked around the side of the garage. He stood for a minute staring at the back door to Mr. Applebaum's house, wishing his friend would appear there just like always with his old brown jacket and rubbers and messy white hair, whistling his song between his teeth. If he would come out now, Jeremy thought, and wink at him, Jeremy would even wink back, a squint-eyed wrinkled-up wink. But no one came, and Jeremy walked slowly down the driveway toward the front of the house.

Even the driveway felt empty. There was nothing in it, not even a car. The paint spots were there, faded but still visible, like bloodstains.

Jeremy cut across the front of the Applebaums'

yard toward his own house, and something up on the front porch caught his eye. It looked like Mr. Applebaum sitting over on the side of the porch, behind the vines that grew up the trellis to the roof. The vines were just beginning to get leafy, and they cast blotchy dark shadows across the porch so it was hard to see, but Jeremy was sure it was his friend.

Jeremy raced up the wooden steps, calling, "Hey, Mr. Applebaum!" Then he stopped short. He'd made a mistake. This man wasn't Mr. Applebaum. He looked like Mr. A., but only in the way his brother might look like him. You could recognize the similarity, but you knew it wasn't the same man. This man sat hunched in an old rocker staring down at the floor. His white hair was trimmed neatly and combed into place, and he wore a stiff pressed white shirt, new clean overalls, and a loose gray sweater.

The man raised his head and a flicker of recognition passed over his face. "Hey, son," he said.

"Mr. Applebaum?" Jeremy asked. He walked closer to the man. It was Mr. Applebaum, he knew. His big old rough hands rested in his lap. The dirt was missing from the cracks and crevices, but those were Mr. Applebaum's hands, the hands that could fix anything, the hands with one finger lost to a tractor years ago.

"I . . . I was out in the garage," Jeremy said. Then he blurted out, "Everything's gone."

Mr. Applebaum didn't say a word. Jeremy wondered if he had heard him.

He was wearing thick clean white socks and no shoes. His feet made a soft sound on the porch floor as he rocked gently. Jeremy found the sound comforting, but he missed Mr. Applebaum's song. He rested his arm on the back of the rocker and became part of the motion. He didn't know what else to do.

"Samuel," a voice called from the front yard. Through the shadowy vines Jeremy could see that it was Mr. Gilbert from across the street. He didn't come up the steps, but he called again from the front walk. "Samuel, can you spare a couple of eggs from your chickens? Milly's making a cake for the grandchildren and she's fresh out of eggs."

Mr. Applebaum shook his head. Jeremy waited for him to answer, but he didn't. So Jeremy called, "The chickens are all gone."

"Now, that's a shame," Mr. Gilbert said as he started back across the street. Then he turned and squinted, trying to get a better view of the porch. "Milly says to say hello, Samuel. Says she hasn't seen you out in a while and she's asking after you." Then he walked away.

"Even the chickens are gone," Jeremy said half to himself. He sat down on a stool next to Mr. Applebaum. "Everything's gone," Jeremy whispered. "They took everything."

It was quiet with only the swooshing of Mr. Applebaum's feet on the porch as he rocked. The soft sound of Mr. Applebaum's voice startled Jeremy.

"I've done led a good, clean, hard-working life," he said. "I never cheated no one as I know of, and I always done the best I knew how. No one's goin' to take that away from me." Mr. Applebaum patted Jeremy's arm as if to comfort him, but he spoke absently and his voice sounded tired.

Jeremy looked up to see if his friend was really talking to him, and Mr. Applebaum winked, a clear, bright, blue-eyed wink. Then he started rocking again.

Jeremy stood up. He wanted to wink back, but when he looked at his friend, the eyes that had winked at him were gone. A gray stare had settled over them again. Jeremy felt like Mr. Applebaum didn't even know he was there.

Jeremy felt a tear form on his eyelash, and there was a lump in his throat. He was embarrassed, and the hollow rhythm of the swooshing and the rocking began to bother him. There was nothing he could say, and even if there was, he couldn't say it now.

Finally he said "See ya" in a strangled voice and ran down the porch steps.

Chapter 16

When Jeremy got to his house, he knew he couldn't go inside, not the way he felt. He didn't want to see anyone, and he didn't feel like going up to his room. He walked up the four cement steps to the front porch and sat heavily on the top step. He felt sick and suddenly very tired, the way Mr. Applebaum looked. But Mr. Applebaum also had looked like he was far away, and that's the part that scared Jeremy most.

Sitting in that rocking chair, Mr. Applebaum had looked all curled up and old. Jeremy had never thought of his friend as an old man. He was just Mr. Applebaum, and he had always been the same age, never old or young. Mr. Applebaum, who could fix anything or make anything. Another tear rolled down Jeremy's cheek.

He wished again for the hundredth time that everything could be the same as it had been just a week or two ago. None of this would have happened, he told himself, if that little kid hadn't been messing around where she wasn't supposed to be. *Or if I had covered up the hole when Mr. Applebaum said to,* he thought miserably, *or if Robbie had never brought those kids here and stolen the paint. How can things get so messed up?* Jeremy wondered. He felt completely helpless.

"Hey, Jeremy." Jeremy looked up to see Robbie was walking up the sidewalk to his house. Just the last person he wanted to see, ever. What was that kid doing here?

Jeremy put his head down and hoped Robbie couldn't see he'd been crying. What gave him the right to just walk up here like nothing had happened? Who did Robbie think he was? Jeremy could hardly breathe, and he felt his face flush with heat.

Robbie was nearly at the bottom step. Before he knew what he was doing, Jeremy sprang from the top step and jumped right on top of Robbie. He had his arms and legs wrapped around him and they both went down sideways onto the grass. Robbie yelled, but his words were broken by the fall. Jeremy was still on top when they hit the ground, and he started punching wildly without thinking about where he could get a good hit or about protecting himself. "You dirty rotten liar," he yelled. "You thief."

Robbie tried to roll Jeremy off. Then he covered his face, and Jeremy heard his muffled protests, but he wasn't listening. He held on, straddling Robbie with his knees and pounding with his fists, while Robbie squirmed and struggled. There was a roaring in Jeremy's ears and he felt as if he would explode. "I hate you," Jeremy croaked. "It's your fault. I know you stole the paint just like you stole the candy bars. You're a thief and a troublemaker." Suddenly he stopped. He was exhausted and his body was limp. He rolled off Robbie and lay in the grass next to him.

Robbie got to his feet. "You finished?" he asked. He offered Jeremy a hand, but Jeremy didn't take it. He sat up, hanging his head between his knees.

"Listen," Robbie said quietly. "I know what you think. But I didn't do it. That's what I came to tell you. I'm cleared. The judge let me go. I didn't do it."

"You expect me to believe that?" Jeremy asked without raising his head. "You stole the candy. You were here with those kids. How did you get off? More lying?" he asked bitterly.

"Look, Jeremy, I wasn't there. Tom finally told

the truth. He got real scared in the court with all that stuff about telling the truth and having it all on your record. His dad had told him to tell the police I showed them where the paint was. They wanted to make it look like it was my idea to do that stuff in town. Then maybe I'd get the worst blame. But Tom got scared in court and told the whole thing. The judge just told me I'd better watch the company I keep and let me go. My mom was crying." He paused a minute. "I guess I cried some, too. Boy, was I relieved."

Jeremy looked at his friend now. "You mean those guys got the paint by themselves?" It was quiet while Jeremy thought about that. "You never should have brought them here, though," he added softly.

"Yeah," Robbie said. "But what's a few cans of paint? I didn't tell them to take it."

That made Jeremy mad again. What did Robbie know? Those kids had ruined his fort, knocked it cockeyed so that little Hull kid could fall in.

"You're still a thief," Jeremy added without vehemence. He wanted to say, "And it's all your fault," but he didn't. If Robbie was telling the truth, then Mr. Applebaum's problems were as much his fault as Robbie's.

Now Robbie lowered his head. "Look, Jeremy, I wanted to talk to you about that. I told my Mom about the candy and all. Really, it's the first time I did it here, and I only did it one other time with my cousin. I got so scared about the police and them talking about juvenile court and juvenile detention and stuff, I told her everything. She went right to Mr. Dickson and told him and made me pay him. And guess what? She says I can have a paper route. She said it would give me some spending money and teach me responsibility and maybe keep me out of trouble, so she's willing to have a trial period." Robbie took a breath. "And I might be able to get a hamster."

Jeremy felt miserable, but he half smiled at his friend. "That's great," he said without much enthusiasm.

"I thought maybe you could help," Robbie said quietly. "I mean, I'd pay you something."

"Sure," Jeremy said. "I gotta go now. My mom doesn't know I'm out here."

"See ya tomorrow," Robbie said.

Jeremy went around to the back door. He needed a few more minutes before he went in.

It looked like Robbie was doing OK. In fact, he didn't have any problems anymore. He had a paper route and he was going to get a pet, while Jeremy couldn't even keep Flash. Robbie seemed to think he and Jeremy could be friends, just like nothing had ever happened. But Jeremy wasn't sure it would ever be the same again, even if Robbie never stole another candy bar. All Jeremy could think about now was Mr. Applebaum and the way he sat in his rocker staring straight ahead.

135

Chapter 17

"Hey, Jeremy, wake up." Andrea was pounding on Jeremy's bedroom door. "Your friend the ex-con is downstairs devouring all the doughnuts."

Jeremy rolled over and stared at the ceiling. He usually got up early on Saturday. Sometimes he even went with Dad to buy doughnuts. But today, he just wanted to stay in bed and forget about everything.

Andrea pounded on the door again, and Jeremy couldn't fall back into the safe, warm half-sleep he had been jolted out of. Besides, Robbie was downstairs, so he knew he had to get up. Robbie.

Robbie, who was supposed to be his best friend, who only a few weeks ago Jeremy would have raced downstairs to greet. Now Jeremy wished he would go away.

When he got to the kitchen, Mom was the only one there. "Where's Robbie?" Jeremy asked, thinking maybe he'd gotten up for nothing.

"He's out in the backyard," Mom said. "I told him to go wake you up, but he said he'd wait outside."

Jeremy passed up the doughnuts. There were only two sugar and cinnamon left, and Jeremy figured Robbie and Andrea had eaten all the glazed and powdered. He downed a glass of orange juice and he could feel it through his whole body. He felt better already.

Stepping out onto the back porch, tentatively, with bare feet, he could feel it was real warm out. Robbie was bent over a big, rusty old red wagon. Jeremy remembered it from when Robbie's mom used to take them to the library in it, or at least he remembered pictures of him and Robbie in it. That was the problem. It seemed all Jeremy's memories were mixed up with Robbie. The good times and the bad.

Robbie stood up. "I pulled this thing out of the garage. I want to fix it up for delivering my papers. I got lucky. Jeff Rawson is going to let me pick up his route. Only problem is it's a few blocks away from my house, and the Sunday papers are heavy. Mom suggested the wagon."

"You sure that thing's going to make it with a load of Sunday papers?" Jeremy asked.

"That's one reason I came," Robbie told him. "I thought maybe Mr. Applebaum would have a new pin and cap for this wheel and maybe a new axle. The handle needs to be straightened, and I could use some paint for the rust. I don't care if it's red or not."

"Yeah." Jeremy couldn't help himself. "The red paint is all gone."

"Come on, Jer. You aren't still mad? I told you I didn't take the paint. I would have never brought those guys by here if I thought . . ."

"Forget it," Jeremy said. He slumped down on the top step. "Anyway, Mr. Applebaum can't help you. Everything's gone."

"What do you mean?"

"When those guys took the paint, they must have messed with my fort. Some little kid from down the street came over and fell in the hole. She broke her arm and the police said Mr. Applebaum had to clean things up."

"All I need is a few little pieces, a hammer, and something we could use for an axle. Come on, let's go ask."

"There's nothing there!" Jeremy shouted. Why wouldn't Robbie listen? "Look," he said, pointing across the hedges.

Robbie stepped up on the bottom step to get a better view. "Wow, is that really Mr. A.'s yard? I see what you mean. What did they do with all that stuff?"

Jeremy told him about the dumpster and the men who had come to take things away. "Mr. Applebaum doesn't fix things anymore," he ended. "He just sits."

"Gosh, Jeremy, Mr. Applebaum can still do repairs, can't he? He doesn't need all that stuff just to fix a wagon."

"I don't know," Jeremy told Robbie. "It's like he's given up or something."

"My dad's uncle has a repair shop. He just works in his basement. People even pay him to fix stuff. He's got some junk around, but nothing like Mr. A. used to have. He fixed my dad's fan in ten minutes when I was there, didn't even need any parts." Robbie took a breath. "Of course, he didn't charge us. My uncle can fix just about anything, stuff most people would throw away."

Jeremy bet Mr. A. could fix anything just as well as Robbie's uncle, better even. He used to fix things for everyone all the time, and he did it for free. He did it because he liked to fix things, the way Jeremy liked to design inventions.

He looked over the hedge. The tools were still there, but there wasn't anything left to fix. Jeremy sighed.

Robbie interrupted his thoughts. "I sure was counting on Mr. Applebaum to fix the wagon. Now what am I going to do? It'll never carry a load of Sunday papers like this."

Jeremy was barely listening. Robbie was right, Mr. Applebaum could still fix things. He couldn't stop fixing things any more than Jeremy could stop trying out his inventions. Mr. Applebaum just needed something to repair.

Jeremy jumped up off the steps and grabbed the handle of Robbie's wagon. "Come on," he said heading down the driveway. "We'll get this wagon fixed."

"How, Jeremy?" Robbie had to run to catch up with him.

"Mr. Applebaum's going to do it. You're right, he doesn't need all that stuff to fix things." The wagon handle was bent, so Jeremy had to stoop down to pull it, and the wheels made a terrible squeaking and scraping noise as the boys headed around the side of the house.

"I hope he's out here," Jeremy said as Robbie came up alongside of him. They turned up Mr. Applebaum's front walk. "There he is," he said a minute later, squinting to see through the vines on the trellis. It seemed like they had grown even thicker just since yesterday. Jeremy rested the handle back, left the wagon at the bottom of the steps, and climbed up.

Mr. Applebaum was sitting just as he had been yesterday in a clean pair of overalls and plaid shirt, only he didn't have the sweater on. "Hey," Jeremy said, half hoping to hear the familiar "Hey, son." Instead, all he heard was the swishing of stocking feet across the porch floor.

Robbie was standing off to the side and behind Jeremy. He spoke up. "Hey, that doesn't look like . . ."

Jeremy gave him an elbow in the gut, just hard enough to shut him up.

"How ya doin'?" Jeremy asked.

"Oh, fine, I expect." Mr. Applebaum spoke in a slow monotone and just kept rocking and looking straight ahead. That gave Jeremy the creeps. Maybe he should forget about the whole idea, he thought, but he was here now and Robbie was standing behind him.

"Robbie's wagon needs to be fixed," Jeremy went on. "We need it 'cause he's getting a new paper route, and he's got to have something to carry his papers in. We thought maybe you could repair it. I know that you don't have all your stuff, but you still got your tools, 'cause I saw them all lined up there in the garage."

Mr. Applebaum didn't say anything, and Jeremy began to think this was a dumb idea.

"Come on, Jeremy." He felt Robbie nudge him in the back. "This is getting nowhere. I see what

141

you mean." Jeremy heard his friend go down the steps to the sidewalk.

Jeremy had an idea. "Well, we'll just leave the wagon here, and if you decide to try and fix it, you can. Robbie really needs it." Jeremy backed down the steps.

"Jeremy, I need that wagon," Robbie hissed. "I can't leave it here."

Jeremy pulled his friend down the front walk and gave him a hard stare that meant *shut up.*

"What if someone takes my wagon?" Robbie asked.

"Nobody's going to take that piece of junk. Besides, we'll keep an eye on it."

"Well, where's he going to get the stuff to fix it?"

"Look," Jeremy said, feeling helpless. "I don't know, but you said it yourself. Mr. A. can fix anything, and he can do it with practically nothing. He just needs a little time."

"I hope you're right. I start my route next week, and I can't do it without that wagon." They had reached Jeremy's front walk.

"Jer, I got to go. I told my mom I'd be home at noon, and I got to be on time for a while."

"I'll keep an eye on the wagon," Jeremy said.

"Thanks," Robbie told him. "I'll call you later. I hope this works."

"It'll work," Jeremy said, but as he went back into the kitchen, he wasn't at all sure. It was like trying to save Flash—you put out the bait, and then you had to wait. Wait and hope.

Dad was sitting at the kitchen table reading the paper. Jeremy noticed both plastic mousetraps were sprung, just sitting in the same places they had been for several days. He picked one up. The peanut butter was still inside, and it looked gross. It seemed like Flash had given up on the traps.

Jeremy hadn't seen Flash lately, and he was a little concerned that something might have happened to him. What if he had chewed on the electrical cords, like Mr. Applebaum said, and got electrocuted, or burned in the stove? Or what if Andrea had gotten ahold of Flash? But Flash was too smart for that. He was too smart to get caught. It was that simple. Jeremy had given up even setting the traps for the last two nights in a row.

Holding the trap, he rocked the door open and closed absentmindedly. It was so simple, just a little tilted box with a door that rocked on two little hooks. Too bad it didn't work. It was too lightweight or something. *We should at least get our money back,* Jeremy thought grimly.

"Find anything out at the pet store yesterday?" Dad asked over the top of the paper.

"Not much," Jeremy said with a long face. "Just that I should try nuts. But the problem isn't *attracting* Flash, or at least it hasn't been. He loves brownies and bananas and toast."

"I think you're right," Dad said. "And I think

we're going to have to get tough with your little friend. Mom is right, too. He could do a job on the wiring. That could get expensive, and I'd hate to see what would happen around here if someone found a mouse in their iced tea." Dad stood up and patted Jeremy on the shoulder. "I couldn't get any help at the hardware store either, but I have to tell you, I picked up some traps, one sticky trap and two of the traditional kind. The man there said he thought the sticky ones worked better but the spring traps were probably more humane since they work faster. I think we should set them this weekend. I'll do it if you'd rather not."

Jeremy didn't argue. He could tell Dad wasn't happy about the traps either, but they'd tried everything. Now there was only a slim hope that Flash would be too smart for the spring traps, too, but Jeremy knew it was only a matter of time before Flash was caught.

*

Jeremy threw himself on his bed, which was where he should have stayed this morning. He rolled over and stared at the ceiling. He squinted one eye and traced in his mind the faint design on the ceiling lamp. If you left out the two flowers, the stems and leaves made a design like a dragon shape. Jeremy had traced it in his mind many times. It looked better in the dark, more like a dragon. It was a good way to get to sleep, just concentrate on that dragon shape and make your mind go over and over the lines. It allowed him to black out everything else.

Jeremy thought maybe he should get up and check out the window for Robbie's wagon, but he was sure Mr. Applebaum was still on his porch and the wagon was still on the sidewalk. What a dumb idea to leave it there. Mr. Applebaum looked like he was never going to get out of that rocking chair again. He looked like he couldn't get out of it. Jeremy sighed. Why didn't he give up? He'd given up on Flash. Dad was setting the spring traps right now. What this world needed was more people like Mr. Applebaum, or at least more people like Mr. Applebaum used to be. And fewer people like Mr. Hull and Tom Morgan.

He rolled over on his stomach and put his head in his hands. *What this world needs is a better mousetrap,* he thought. He reached out and slid his drawing pad and pencil off the bedside table. Doodling on the paper without even thinking, Jeremy realized he had drawn a mouse. Flash. How could he let Flash be killed in a spring trap or a sticky trap? There just had to be a better way.

Jeremy tried to think of all the ways he knew about to trap animals. After all, what did zoos do? They needed to capture animals alive. They weren't all born in captivity. Maybe they could drug Flash, put him in a cage, and let him go when he woke up. What did you use to drug a mouse, and how much of it, and how did you get close enough to inject it? Unless, of course, you fed him a pill, but how could you make sure Flash would eat it? Scratch that idea.

What about a trap that Flash would step into and then a rope—or in a mouse's case a string—would snare him, like a lasso? He'd have to trip something that would pull the string. Jeremy started sketching his ideas. Something to do with weights and pulleys might work. But Jeremy could see that would be too complicated and not exact enough. He didn't want to end up hanging Flash, after all.

What about a cage that dropped down over Flash when he tripped the string? That was better. Jeremy drew another sketch. That idea had drawbacks, too. What if the cage came down on Flash instead of over him and knocked him out or something?

"Hey, Jeremy, you in there?" Andrea was calling from outside the bedroom door. Jeremy noticed she hadn't been calling him Squirt lately. Maybe there was hope for his sister.

"What do you want?" he called without moving from the bed.

Andrea poked her head in the door. "I see Dad

146

is setting those spring traps. Looks like Flash is doomed. Just wanted to tell you I was sorry."

"Yeah, thanks," Jeremy said. Andrea really was getting nice. "He's not caught yet and I'm still trying to come up with something. What do you think about this?" Jeremy held out his sketches.

Andrea came into the room and took the notebook from Jeremy. "Cute mouse," she said, "but the traps look pretty complicated. Let's face it, Jeremy, Flash is on his way out."

Andrea had her hand on the doorknob. "I was hoping you might consider donating his body to science. I mean, it would be a good cause, furthering the goals of modern science and all."

For a minute, Jeremy didn't know what she was talking about. Then he understood and picked up a shoe and aimed it at his sister. "Get out of here," he yelled. The shoe hit the closed door with a loud thud.

"Just thought I'd ask," Andrea's voice came through the door. "We get to do a crayfish next week. Mr. Carson said he got the shipment in yesterday."

So Andrea was going to dissect a crayfish. You'd think that would satisfy her need to cut things up, but she still wanted Flash. Somehow a crayfish didn't seem as bad as a furry little warm creature like Flash.

He wondered idly how they caught crayfish,

anyway. Maybe they used nets or something like a lobster trap. Lobster pots, they were called. Jeremy had seen them when they went to Maine for vacation. They were so simple—slatted wooden cages with bait in them. A fisherman had shown Jeremy how they worked. There was a hole in the trap made out of woven rope. It was wide on the outside and narrow on the inside, so when the lobster went in the wide end to get the bait, he couldn't get out again through the narrow end.

Perfect. That's what Jeremy needed for Flash, a trap he could get into but not out of again. He started sketching. The hole didn't have to be made of rope, maybe string or wire. The cage could be made out of screen or chicken wire, like Mr. Applebaum had in his garage. *Or used to have*, Jeremy corrected himself.

Even the thought of Mr. Applebaum's empty garage didn't stop Jeremy. He knew he could get the wire somewhere. But the thought of Mr. A. did remind Jeremy about Robbie's wagon. He jumped off his bed and pulled back the window curtain. The peak of the roof of Mr. A.'s house filled the view from Jeremy's bedroom window, but if he stood way off to the side of the window and looked down at an angle, he could see just about all the way up Mr. Applebaum's front walk, almost to the steps. The wagon was gone. Or at least he couldn't see it. That meant one of two things. Someone had taken Robbie's wagon, or Mr. Applebaum had fallen for the bait.

Jeremy had to find out right away. He grabbed his notebook, stuffed his feet into his sneakers, and raced down the stairs.

Chapter 18

Jeremy half expected the wagon still to be there when he came around the side of the house. Probably he just couldn't get a good view from upstairs, he told himself. Probably Mr. A. was still sitting staring at it. But what if it was gone? What if it was gone and Mr. A. was still there? What was he going to tell Robbie?

Sure enough, the wagon was gone. Jeremy practically held his breath and tiptoed toward the front porch. It looked like Mr. Applebaum was gone, too. Jeremy was almost afraid to look too closely through the trellis and the shadows it cast. Still, he needed to make sure. The rocking chair was definitely empty. Jeremy almost cheered. Mr. A. had taken the bait. But it wasn't a trap Jeremy had set for his friend. More like showing the way to freedom, he hoped—the same thing he had to do for Flash.

Jeremy headed toward Mr. Applebaum's garage. Inside, Jeremy's eyes had to adjust to the dim light, and this time his brain had to adjust, too. He had forgotten how neat and clean it was now. There was Mr. Applebaum, all right, at the end of the garage between the front of the car and the workbench. He was just as neat and clean as the garage, but Jeremy noticed with relief that instead of white stocking feet, he had on the same old worn leather shoes with black rubbers over them that Jeremy was used to. He was bent over Robbie's wagon, which was standing up on end so he could work on the front axle and handle.

"Hey," Jeremy said quietly.

"Humph," Mr. A. said without looking up. "This wagon don't need much work at all. Nothing that can't be fixed with a few good tools. Needs a good coat of paint, too."

Jeremy moved closer to examine his friend's work. "Where'd you get the new axle?"

"Just straightened the old one."

"What about the pin and cap for the wheel?"

"I still got me a few things left in the basement."

"That's great," Jeremy said.

"Now, what'd I do with that blame hammer?" Mr. Applebaum grumbled. "Clean a place up and a feller can't never find nothing."

Jeremy laughed. Mr. A. was sounding more like himself every minute. "Isn't that your hammer there, hanging in its place?"

"How do you suppose the dang thing got there?" Mr. A. asked, banging the pin into place on the axle. He set the wagon down. "Try it out, son."

"It's great," Jeremy called. He wheeled the wagon out of the garage.

Mr. Applebaum followed him. "Guess I got some paint in the basement if you boys want to give it a coat before it rusts away." Mr. Applebaum headed toward the house. Jeremy wondered if he should go after him, but then his friend stopped and stood with his hands on his hips, staring out at the garden. Jeremy left the wagon and stood beside him.

There were little green shoots popping up everywhere. Some weren't so little anymore. There were even a few on the fresh soil that filled in the hole where Jeremy's fort had been.

"Humph," Mr. A. said again.

"I could help weed it for you," Jeremy offered. "If you show me what's weeds."

"I was just thinking those new seedlings from under the hothouse need to be set out, but

152

those blame chipmunks will have them finished off in no time unless I take care of them." Mr. Applebaum thought for a minute and sighed a short huffy sigh. "I expect my traps are gone with everything else."

Traps. Jeremy remembered now. Mr. Applebaum had told him that he always had to catch the chipmunks in his garden. He didn't kill them. He let them go up in the field or somewhere. "Hey," Jeremy said, "what kind of traps?"

"Aw, just something I rigged up," Mr. Applebaum mumbled, and his eyes got the glassy stare that worried Jeremy.

"Look, Mr. Applebaum, I got this idea for a trap." He held out his drawing pad, which he had been carrying since he left his room. Mr. Applebaum looked at it, but Jeremy couldn't tell if he was really seeing it. Jeremy was excited and nervous at the same time. "Mom found out about Flash. He's my secret pet mouse. Remember? Now she says I have to get rid of him. We tried those store-bought traps that catch a mouse alive, but Flash is too darn smart. My dad is setting a spring trap for him right now. I have to think of another way to catch Flash. Before it's too late," he added. "I tried to draw some ideas."

Mr. Applebaum was quiet, but he was looking down at Jeremy's drawings, and Jeremy could tell he was interested. Finally, his mouth turned up slightly at the corners. He took the pad in both of

153

his big rough hands. "What's this?" He pointed to the lobster trap design.

"Just an idea I had," Jeremy told him. "I thought if the mouse went in to get the bait, then when he tried to get out, the hole, which is supposed to be funnel shaped, would be too small."

"I'll be." Mr Applebaum actually chuckled. "I'll be darned if that's not the same trap I use to catch me my chipmunks."

Jeremy smiled, too. "Like a lobster trap."

Mr. A. just nodded. He was already on his way back toward the house. "Come on, son. We got us some work to do. We'll find some paint for that wagon, too."

Jeremy followed Mr. A.'s big solid form that was just a little stooped now as he took slow but sturdy steps into his house. Jeremy had never been inside before, and he hesitated behind his friend holding the screen door open, hoping he wouldn't have to see Mrs. Applebaum.

The doorway opened into a tiny square hallway that led off to the right down steep gray wooden steps to the basement. There were no backs to the steps, and he could see the basement floor between each step. Jeremy walked slowly, holding on to the railing on one side and steadying himself with his other hand on the wall. He looked down at his feet to make sure he didn't miss a step in the dim light.

He felt better when he got to the solid red

brown cement floor and Mr. Applebaum pulled the string to the light bulb overhead. "Wow," Jeremy exclaimed.

Mr. Applebaum's basement looked almost like his garage. Or at least the way his garage used to look. There was stuff everywhere—boxes and crates, ropes, ladders, skis, ski poles, and snowshoes. There was even a chair, without any seat to it, hanging from the ceiling.

"Let's see now," Mr. Applebaum said as he started collecting wire and screen. "Pick out a couple dozen nails about half as long as your little finger." He handed Jeremy an old wooden box full of screws and nails and nuts and bolts. "I expect I got some wood here somewheres."

After Jeremy picked out a pocketful of nails, Mr. Applebaum told him to find some paint for the wagon. He pointed to a stack of old paint cans in a corner. Some of the cans were dried up, but Jeremy found one with bright-green paint dripping down the sides that felt at least half full when he shook it. Jeremy wondered what Robbie would say about a green wagon. Come to think of it, Jeremy had never seen any other color wagon besides red before. Why were wagons always red? But he knew Robbie wouldn't care if his wagon was green. It was so old, any color would be OK.

When they had collected what they needed for the traps, Jeremy and Mr. Applebaum carried it all back to the garage. Jeremy sawed a piece of wood for the bottom of the trap, and Mr. Applebaum helped him nail the wire screen on in an arch to make the top and sides. They bent some screen and cut it with wire cutters to fit in the ends. Then they cut a hole in one side and made a funnel-shaped entrance with the large opening on the outside. Mr. Applebaum showed Jeremy how to wire one end to make a door.

Jeremy looked at what they had done so far. The funnel opening was made out of wire, not string or rope like Jeremy had in his design or the way a lobster trap might be.

"I think Flash would be able to fit back out through that opening," Jeremy told Mr. Applebaum.

"Well, we're not finished yet." Mr. Applebaum helped Jeremy put some sharp barbed wires on the inside of the funnel, so once Flash got inside the trap, he wouldn't want to try to get out the narrow opening with barbs. They bent a piece of wire and attached it to the top of the trap for a handle.

Jeremy held up the finished trap to admire. "It's great. Just what I'd planned."

"Think you'll catch yourself a mouse, do you?" Mr. Applebaum chuckled and Jeremy knew he felt as good as Jeremy did. It felt great to build something like that, to have an idea and work on it and get it to come out right. That's what had been so great about Mr. Applebaum's garage. All those things, all those ideas and possibilities.

Suddenly, Jeremy didn't feel so good about his trap. Mr. A. had fixed the wagon, but now what? There was nothing left.

"What's the matter, son? Cat got your tongue?"

"It's gone. Everything's gone," Jeremy blurted out. "I, I'm sorry," he stammered. "I didn't fill in the fort when you told me to. If I'd filled in the fort, that kid would never have fallen in, and none of this would have happened. It's all my fault."

"Well now," Mr. Applebaum said, "you must think you're pretty important to be the cause of so much trouble." He paused, resting a hand on Jeremy's shoulder, and then added, "No, blame ain't usually that simple. But in this case, I get the biggest share, I'm afraid." Then he smiled. "Don't you worry none. I still got me two good hands. Proved that on your wagon, didn't I?" He winked at Jeremy. "What's the matter—don't you think my place is pretty enough now?"

Jeremy managed a halfhearted smile and shrugged. "It's not bad, I guess." At least Mr. Applebaum seemed OK.

It was nearly dinnertime when they finished the trap. Mr. Applebaum walked out of the garage with Jeremy. "Good to see you out and about, Samuel," Mr. Abbottello called from the side fence and waved. "Been a little worried about you."

Mr. Applebaum put his hand up in greeting. "No need to worry." Jeremy looked at his new trap and thought maybe, just maybe, there wasn't any reason to worry about Mr. Applebaum or Flash.

Walking home, Jeremy decided the best place for the trap would probably be near the stove. He hoped Mom and Dad would consider giving the new trap a try. He hoped they would think it was as brilliant as he did.

Then Jeremy had a terrible thought. What if he was too late? He had been over at Mr. Applebaum's for two hours at least. What if Flash was already caught? Jeremy quickened his pace. He should have told Dad to wait. He had finally solved the problem, and now it was all going to be for nothing.

He was half afraid to go in the back door. In one quick glance, he could see that both spring traps were empty, but still set. Jeremy immediately relaxed enough to notice that Dad was preparing dinner.

"Great," Jeremy said. "Tacos. Dad, look what Mr. Applebaum helped me make." He held the mouse trap up by the handle.

Dad looked over his shoulder as he popped the tacos into the oven. "Let me guess. A tarantula cage?"

"Come on, Dad. It's a mousetrap. A better mousetrap," he said proudly. He showed his father how it was supposed to work. "I'm going to put bananas and peanut butter inside."

"Looks like it might work," Dad said. "We'll give it a try, anyway. I must say, I was beginning to feel bad about doing Flash in. We'll have to deactivate those other traps."

"Sure," Jeremy said. "I'll do it." He set down his trap and grabbed one of the spring traps. Snap! The sound was earsplitting. "Wow," Jeremy yelled, dropping the trap on the floor. He shook his hand automatically, even though the trap hadn't gotten him.

"I should have warned you," Dad said. "Those traps are sensitive."

Jeremy shook his head in agreement and in wonder at the thought of what such a device could do to Flash.

As soon as everything was quiet in the kitchen, Jeremy positioned his trap. He dropped a slice of banana with peanut butter inside, and then, because they had had Flash's favorite treat for dessert that night, he added a quarter of a brownie. Jeremy thought about trying to stay up to watch for Flash, but he didn't want to do anything to ruin the possibility that his new trap would do the trick. Mom had agreed that it was a clever idea and worth a try, but she'd warned him that they would have to go back to the spring trap if Jeremy's didn't work soon.

Chapter 19

It was early when Jeremy woke up on Sunday. When he realized it was not a school day, he was about to roll over and fade back into a sound sleep, but the memory of Flash and his new trap jerked him awake again. He was wearing shorts and the same big blue T-shirt he always wore to bed, and he didn't even bother to put on a bathrobe before racing downstairs.

Please be there, Flash. Please be there. Jeremy sent a silent message to his pet as he entered the kitchen.

The trap was immediately visible from the doorway but Jeremy had to move closer to be completely sure. "Holy smoke," he whispered to

160

himself, and took a second look to confirm what he had seen. Two tails, two heads, and eight tiny paws. Two gray-and-pink mice, each a mirror image of the other! They both sat perfectly still looking out at Jeremy. Jeremy was so close he could detect a little tremble in each of their bodies.

"Flash?" Jeremy said almost in a whisper. Both mice started and went down on all fours again to stay motionless. "Which one of you guys is Flash? Maybe you're both Flash," he answered for himself. He shook his head. Wait until Mom found out they had two mice!

Jeremy stared at the two tiny creatures and they stared back. It didn't really matter which one was Flash. "You guys are both safe now, even if you don't think so," he told them.

"No wonder Flash got into so much mischief," Dad said when he came down. "There are two of him."

"Have you figured out which one is the female?" Andrea wanted to know.

"How do you know one is a female?" Jeremy asked.

"I just figured if there are two, one is probably a male and one a female. If Flash is the male, then you could let him go and maybe I could have the other one."

"No way." Jeremy cradled the trap protectively. The two mice were exactly alike, and there was no way he could tell which one was Flash.

"That trap is more like a cage," Andrea pointed out. "Maybe you could keep them as pets."

Jeremy looked at the two mice. They were circling the trap and standing up to examine the wire every few seconds. They were looking for a way out, Jeremy knew. He didn't want a pet that wasn't free. "No," he told Andrea. "Flash shouldn't be in a cage. I have to let them go."

Dad made pancakes and Jeremy ate a stack of five. He tore one up in tiny pieces for Flash and his friend, but the mice didn't eat anything.

Dad offered to go up the street to the cemetery with Jeremy, but he wanted to be by himself when he set Flash free.

*

He walked in through the cemetery gates and down the cement path knowing just where he was going to let his friends out. There was a little pond off to one side, away from the gravestones and down from the flower garden. It was overgrown with weeds and long grasses. Jeremy figured Flash could find a place to hide where there would be some seeds and berries and plenty of water.

Gently, Jeremy set the trap down in some grass and old leaves. Then he opened the door on the opposite side from the trap entrance.

Both mice stood still for a minute. Neither of them darted out as Jeremy had expected them to

162

do. "Go ahead, guys," he said, tipping the trap a bit to shake them out. They tumbled over each other. Jeremy watched for a few minutes as they explored and sat up and listened and looked. He laughed, remembering how fast they had been in the kitchen, how they'd earned the name Flash. *More like Pokey,* he thought now. "I guess it's kind of scary being out in the big world," he said as both mice disappeared under the leaves and grass. He picked up the trap. "I guess it will take you guys a little while to get used to your new home. Bye." He hoped they would be safe there. At least they were safe from spring traps and Andrea.

Jeremy couldn't wait to get back to Mr. Applebaum's and tell him about how the trap worked, and that Flash was really two mice instead of one.

When Mr. Applebaum heard Jeremy's story, his face wrinkled up into a big grin. "Well, I'll be," he said.

Then Robbie rode up on his bike ready to paint the wagon, and he had to hear the story, too.

"That's great, Jer. I'm glad old Flash is safe. Both of him."

Jeremy grinned. "Too bad you never got to meet him. Or them, I mean."

"Yeah," Robbie agreed. "But at least he's free. It was a close call—and for me, too."

"I heard those other guys got suspended for

two weeks, and they have to see a counselor and pay for the damage," Jeremy said.

"Yeah, I was lucky I wasn't involved. The candy bar thing was bad enough."

Jeremy didn't say anything.

"I guess you're still mad about that. Listen Jer, I'm sorry. I know I could have gotten you into trouble, too."

Jeremy felt like he was supposed to say it was OK. The words stuck in his throat and he stared at the ground. It wasn't OK. Finally, he looked up and said, "I accept your apology." He said it without really feeling it.

"At first I was sure you would tell," Robbie went on. "You're always such a goody-goody. You never do anything wrong. My mom is always getting on me. 'Why can't you be more like Jeremy? Jeremy never uses that kind of language. Jeremy's always home on time.' I knew you'd be scared, and if I got caught, you would too."

Jeremy felt as if he'd been hit. All this time he and Robbie had been best friends, and he never knew Robbie felt like that.

He lowered his eyes and stammered, "I *was* scared, and I did almost tell. I thought maybe I should have after . . . after all the other trouble." Jeremy's voice came out hoarse.

"I guess I wanted you to get into trouble," Robbie continued. "I wanted the great Jeremy to get into trouble. 'See, Mom, even Jeremy, whose dad lives at home and eats dinners with the family every night—even he can be bad.' "

Jeremy kicked at a pebble with the toe of his sneaker. Finally he spoke. "Gosh, Robbie, you have it all wrong. I'm always getting into trouble for arguing with Andrea or daydreaming when I'm supposed to be doing my homework or something. My mom even got upset because of Flash."

"Maybe," Robbie said. "But I don't think it's the same. Anyway"—he smiled—"I should have known you wouldn't tell. I should have known you wouldn't tattle on a friend." Robbie stuck his right hand out awkwardly toward Jeremy. "Shake?"

Jeremy reached out slowly. He was surprised at the firmness of Robbie's grasp, but it felt good. It felt like he and Robbie were really friends again for the first time since Robbie had gotten back from his dad's. Just then he felt closer to Robbie than he ever had before. In spite of everything, Jeremy thought, or maybe because of it.

Robbie broke the silence. "The wagon looks great, Jer. Let's paint."

Mr. Applebaum was busy in the garden and he left the two boys to work by themselves. Green turned out to be a great color for a wagon. They decided a green wagon was going to be Robbie's trademark.

"Mr. A. seemed OK," Robbie remarked as they were finishing up. "I would have never believed it, yesterday."

"I know," Jeremy agreed. "Your wagon did the trick."

Mom and Dad were in the kitchen when Jeremy got home. "Hope you still have that trap," Dad said.

"Why? What's up?" Jeremy asked.

Mom answered, "I spent all morning cleaning these drawers and the stove and I just came in here now and will you look at what I see?" She opened the drawer to show him a small piece of sticky pancake and some mouse droppings in with the silverware.

"Gee, Mom. Are you sure?"

"Of course I'm sure. I put clean drawer liners in and everything."

"Maybe we've got *three* Flashes," Jeremy told her. "I'll set the trap again tonight."

*

Two weeks later, Jeremy and Robbie were over at Mr. Applebaum's finishing up their go-cart. They'd gotten most of the stuff they needed from Mr. Applebaum's basement, and Robbie had brought some things from home. They had worked on the go-cart every day after school before Robbie had to do the papers. Jeremy usually helped with the papers so they would have more time to work. It was turning out even better than Jeremy had imagined it when Robbie was away.

Jeremy left Robbie working in the driveway and ran back to the garage for a hammer. He stopped to watch Mr. Applebaum, who was bent over the workbench, fixing Mr. Abbottello's air conditioner. His white hair was getting shaggy again. The garage was beginning to look cluttered too. Tools all over the place, paint cans and bits of wire and scraps of metal, nails and screws. It felt good to be there. The new rule at Applebaum's was that everything had to fit back in the garage at the end of the day. That meant Mr. Applebaum didn't collect things anymore, at least nothing big. But he always had something to work on.

Jeremy was headed back out to Robbie and the go-cart when he heard someone call, "Samuel, Samuel." It sounded like it was coming from the garden, so Jeremy went around the side of the garage. Sure enough, old Mrs. Sullivan was leaning on the back fence. Mr. Applebaum appeared through the side door of the garage.

Now what does she want? Jeremy wondered. *Hope it's not a complaint.* "There you are, Samuel. The garden is lookin' right nice," she said brightly. Then she hesitated, looking at Jeremy and back to Mr. Applebaum. "Ahh, I was wondering . . ." She stopped again as Robbie came around the side of the garage. Lowering her voice she continued, "I have a kind of a problem with some rodents in my house."

"You say rodents, do you? You don't mean you've got rats living over there?"

Jeremy and Robbie grinned at each other.

"Heavens, no. It's a mouse is all. I was wondering if you have any mousetraps."

"Well, now," Mr. Applebaum said. "I don't, but Jeremy here does." He winked at the boys. "He built himself a trap that caught him six mice in a week."

"Is that so?" Mrs. Sullivan asked suspiciously.

"Sure," Jeremy said. "Twice, we even caught two together. We haven't caught any or seen signs of more mice for almost a week. I've stopped setting the trap."

Mrs. Sullivan frowned. "Some kind of homemade contraption isn't really what I had in mind."

Mr. Applebaum patted Jeremy on the shoulder. "This boy's mousetrap is better than any trap you could buy. But suit yourself."

"I guess it don't do no harm to try," Mrs. Sullivan said.

"I'll bring it over soon as we're finished here," Jeremy told her.

"Maybe you'll catch six or seven of them critters," Mr. Applebaum added. "Maybe even a rat or two." He chuckled and winked at Jeremy. Jeremy laughed too, and this time he winked back.

DATE DUE

HQ CHILDRENS
478138
Williams, Karen Lynn.
Applebaum's garage / by Kare
n Lynn Williams.

DATE DUE	BORROWER'S NAME